THE LIVING RIVER

Liz Johnstone took for granted that all families were as stable and loving as her own. She realised some were not when the mother of Keith Watson, whom she had secretly idolised since her schooldays, staged a well-planned disappearance. Then the new neighbours, elegant Eleanor Martin and daughter June, entered Liz's life and work. She glimpsed a sophistication and confidence that was new and exciting in the narrow mid-thirties life of a ship-building community.

BARBARA COWAN

THE LIVING RIVER

Complete and Unabridged

LINFORD
Leicester

First published in Great Britain in 1997

First Linford Edition
published 2005

British Library CIP Data

Cowan, Barbara
   The living river.—Large print ed.—
Linford romance library
   1. Love stories
   2. Large type books
   I. Title
   823.9′2 [F]

ISBN 1–84395–589–X

Published by
F. A. Thorpe (Publishing)
Anstey, Leicestershire

Set by Words & Graphics Ltd.
Anstey, Leicestershire
Printed and bound in Great Britain by
T. J. International Ltd., Padstow, Cornwall

This book is printed on acid-free paper

A Busy Monday . . .

It was 7.45 a.m. on a fine May morning in 1935. Crowds of workmen, wearing battered, oil-stained cloth caps, and dingy three-piece suits which had once been their best, strolled towards Burnham's shipbuilding yard on the Clyde. Most had 'piece' tins under their arms, others carried clean, rolled-up overalls, for this was Monday. Tram-cars lumbered up and down Dumbarton Road.

From the bay window of her big room in Yarrowholm Street, Esther Johnstone looked down on the busy scene three floors beneath her. She watched Robbie, her husband, walk down the sloping street. It had been her daily ritual since she'd come to Glasgow as a bride, twenty-six years before.

He had been her knight in shining armour then, rescuing her from the

1

drudgery of scullery work in a big house down the coast at Skelmorlie. How she'd hated it, and how wonderful when Robbie Johnstone, the young shipyard plater, had come on holiday during the Glasgow Fair, and they'd fallen in love.

Now she smiled as he paused at the small triangle of garden separating Yarrowholm Street from Dumbarton Road. He made a slight turn towards her, and one finger touched the skip of his cloth cap. He had done that, too, for the last twenty-six years. At the kerb he stood, waiting with a growing crowd of men until a gap came in the traffic and they crossed over, disappearing in a swarm round the next corner to the shipyards on the banks of the river at Scotstoun.

Esther became aware of Liz, her eldest, neat and slim beside her. She turned, choosing her words carefully.

'Now don't be disappointed if you don't get the promotion. You've done well at twenty-five to be Burnham's book-keeper.'

'And I can do better. Why shouldn't I get the job? I've acted secretary to the managing director for the past seven weeks,' Liz Johnstone said lightly. After all, she'd studied hard at night school for her book-keeping 'City & Guilds', then gone on to get good shorthand and typing certificates.

Then her eye lighted on the wonderfully elegant widow Mrs Eleanor Martin, their new English neighbour, walking down the street beneath them. She and her daughter had just moved into the bottom flat in the close.

Compared to the finery of their clothes, their frugal food shopping arrangements raised eyebrows among the other housewives in the close.

'Look at her lovely swagger coat! And the up-tilted brim of her hat matches!' Liz observed. She admired style.

Her mother leaned forward, watching the figure of the graceful woman.

'I wonder where she's going at this time in the morning?' she mused.

They saw the tall figure of Keith

3

Watson running along, losing himself in the swarm of men getting off trams at the Scotstoun West bridge. His father followed, walking with his head held high.

'I've never seen that father and son walk to work together — it's not natural,' Esther commented, shaking her head. In her view the Watsons from the flat below were a strange family.

Liz didn't reply, for she was watching Keith's tall, fair-haired figure among the crush of men heading for Burnham's. When he was out of sight she turned away with a little sigh. She'd secretly idolised him since school, when he was her protector, a big boy, two years ahead of her.

'Well, I'm off, Mum. Mr Nigel asked if I'd come in early. This is the day when the secretary's position will be decided — in my favour, I hope.'

As Liz fixed on her beret in front of the overmantel mirror above the fireplace, Esther gently tried to temper her enthusiasm.

'I'd be surprised if Burnham's want someone with just seven weeks' experience,' she warned, 'no matter how efficient you are.'

'It won't be the end of the world if I don't get it. But I'd like the extra salary. I could start saving.' Liz buttoned her coat. 'I could buy the material I'd need to copy that swagger coat our new neighbour was wearing.'

But Liz kept secret her main reason — that she wanted a change from account books. She'd found the secretary's work interesting, and Mr Burnham, the managing director, was a good boss — unlike his cousin Mr 'Nippy' Nigel Burnham, who always wanted figures half an hour before it was possible.

She dropped a light-hearted kiss on her mother's cheek, and was off.

Esther listened to her footsteps as she ran down the three flights of stairs, then she watched Liz hurry down the slope just as Burnham's horn blew for the start of work and almost immediately the muffled clamour of hammer on metal reached her ears.

She frowned. There was little chance Liz would get that position, for all her hopes.

With a sigh she fetched the metal polish from the lobby press. Burnishing the brass door-handle, letter-box and name-plate on the front door was her next task of the morning.

As she rubbed, reflecting on Liz, the door opposite opened and Olive McDonald, her cheerful neighbour, bustled out with her cleaning cloths.

'I think I'll get my brasses electro-plated to save doing this every morning,' Olive suggested as they worked side by side.

Esther would have liked the new fashion too, but she needed every penny to run the house. Andrew, her eldest boy, was in fifth year medicine at Glasgow University. He'd won a bursary for his fees, but the family had to pay for his books and general upkeep. It was a struggle, for the twins were still apprentices. Luckily there was Liz's wage.

The two women were still polishing their door brasses companionably when they heard the familiar footsteps of the postman on the stairs. The postie had a mischievous glint in his eye.

'Here you are, Mrs McDonald, another one from your boyfriend in Canada! A nice thick one this time.'

'He's no boyfriend of mine!' Olive McDonald muttered under her breath as she thrust the envelope, unopened, into the pocket of her wrap-round apron.

'I didn't know you had connections in Canada,' Esther remarked.

'No connections I'd want to have,' Olive returned, and sniffed, feeling she'd given away too much already about the thick envelope with the foreign stamp.

Esther was puzzled. Her neighbour was usually open and confiding, but the arrival of the letter had made her secretive.

The door on the landing immediately below opened and Keith Watson's

7

mother came upstairs. Normally she kept herself to herself.

'Here it is! What you've been waiting for,' Olive said, handing over the newly-delivered letter, and in the sudden silence, Esther immediately sensed she was intruding.

'Well, must get on,' she said brightly and gathered up her polishing cloths. She would finish the job later.

As she closed the door behind her she couldn't help hearing snatches of the women's conversation and she frowned, somehow uneasy. What was Olive McDonald up to with Mrs Watson?

It was ten years since Olive's husband had died, leaving the corner shop to Olive and their three girls. It provided them with a good income.

Esther shrugged as she put away her cleaning things. She'd hear about it soon enough. Olive McDonald couldn't keep a secret for long.

★   ★   ★

The Burnham Shipbuilding Company's offices took up the whole floor above the time-office, and Liz Johnstone felt excited as she pushed open the half-glazed door with 'Office' engraved on the glass. Somehow, she knew this would be an unusual day.

The high Victorian desks were empty of staff and Liz was about to hurry to the cloakroom when Mr Nigel Burnham's head appeared from the door of his cashier's room.

'Good. I knew I could depend on you to come in early.' He smiled thinly, his black hair plastered smoothly to his head. 'Come in, there's someone here you must meet.'

Liz went uncertainly to the door, and when she saw the other person in the room she had to look twice. It was her new neighbour, standing poised and calm.

'Miss Johnstone, this is Mrs Martin, whom the managing director has personally employed as his secretary.' The cashier's tone was edged with frost. He was offended at not being consulted.

A huge lump of disappointment rose in her throat, and Liz gulped. Swallowing hard, she fought to match Mrs Martin's composure, and held out her hand.

'I'm very pleased to meet you, Mrs Martin. We're neighbours. You've already met my mother.'

'Yes, of course, you must be Liz.' Eleanor Martin shook hands, unaware that Mr Nigel abhorred first names among the office staff.

'Miss Johnstone . . . ' he paused for emphasis ' . . . has been acting secretary for the last seven weeks, so she can explain your duties.'

'Oh, how wonderful. So often one is expected to take over without help.' Mrs Martin smiled eagerly. 'So, Miss Johnstone, if you'll show me where to put my coat and hat, we can make a start.'

Liz glanced at Mr Nigel, for it seemed Mrs Martin had neatly excluded him.

And from the look on his face, he felt the same.

'Good grief! A cupboard with a window!' The new secretary looked with humorous distaste at the narrow cloakroom — a wash-basin under the window, and a small, discoloured mirror fastened to the window-frame.

She hung her coat on a peg while Liz quietly did the same, trying not to think of her lost promotion, although the disappointment crushed her like a huge weight.

'I gather from the cashier that he would have promoted you,' Mrs Martin observed. 'I know it must be frustrating having a stranger like me brought in, but I hope we can be friends.'

Liz looked away quickly, for the other's unexpected sympathy brought a tear to her eye.

'It wasn't a foregone conclusion,' she managed a little stiffly.

Mrs Martin was peering into the mirror, touching up her lipstick and tucking escaping wisps of her hair into grips.

'I see,' she returned. 'Then let's get started.'

It was soon apparent that the new employee was well up to the task — but her near flippancy alarmed Liz. Mrs Martin didn't seem to realise that being Mr Burnham's secretary was a prized post and gave the holder a unique status in the office.

'I suppose it was too much to expect an electric typewriter,' Eleanor Martin murmured, examining her machine.

'It's the best in the office.' Liz frowned, for it was their most up-to-date piece of office equipment.

Now Eleanor Martin was looking speculatively around.

'Are there any spare rooms? The managing director's secretary doesn't usually sit in a corner of the outer office.' She gestured to her desk. 'I'm under the gaze of that tetchy cashier here.'

Liz gasped at the request.

'Only Mr Nigel and Mr Burnham have private rooms,' she explained, indicating the two open doors opposite, and she suddenly realised for the first time how small and shabby they were.

'They certainly don't spend the profits making the office staff comfortable,' was Eleanor Martin's final comment as she took her seat at the typewriter.

Liz knew the yard always got the best equipment and she'd never questioned the furnishings or layout of the office. She'd just accepted that, as book-keeper, she sat on a tall stool at the long Victorian desk, beside the cost clerk, with his two assistants, Will and Bobby, facing on the opposite side. The three McDonald girls from across the land-ing, who were tracers, sat at the drawing boards under the window.

But she didn't have time to ponder as the staff were drifting in for the nine o'clock start. They all paused as they came through the swing door, immedi-ately aware of the new figure at the secretary's desk, red-tipped fingers flying over the keyboard. Bleakly Liz acknowledged to herself that the speed

13

was far in advance of her own.

Accepting the inevitable, she pulled down the purchases ledger from the brass rack above her desk, put her head down and concentrated on the lines of figures.

Just as she had completed a particularly tricky trial balance, she heard the cashier's querulous voice calling from his room, 'Miss Johnstone, please!'

With a sigh Liz climbed down from her stool and went in.

Departing from years of custom, he closed the door behind her.

'Miss Johnstone, you were my candidate for secretary, but my cousin has chosen differently.' He sniffed. 'His privilege, of course. But I feel Mrs Martin doesn't realise that I head the commercial office . . .'

He suddenly lunged to the door and flung it open, and stood bristling with annoyance. Eleanor Martin was going round the newly-arrived office staff, introducing herself to them.

'Miss Johnstone, please tell Mrs

Martin to return to her desk and I will introduce her to all the staff at nine-fifteen.'

Liz stared at him, wanting to refuse, but of course she couldn't, and she felt awkward as she reluctantly went back to the outer office.

Fortunately Mr Burnham, the managing director, breezed in at that moment, still with his overcoat on.

'Ah good! You've arrived, Mrs Martin. Bring the mail to my room in five minutes, will you?'

Once he'd gone, Eleanor Martin turned to Liz.

'Where is the mail?' she asked.

'Mr Nigel's been opening it . . . ' Liz started.

Mrs Martin sighed. 'I see I'm going to have trouble with him.'

She walked purposefully to his office and her knuckles barely touched the open door before she walked in.

Will Robertson and Bobby Douglas, who shared the desk with Liz, were enthralled, as were the female staff, and the office was silent as everyone strained to make out the muffled conversation beyond the closed door.

After a moment Mrs Martin sailed out, her arms full of mail.

'Thank you so much, Mr Nigel. You've been most helpful,' she gushed. 'And I'll see you aren't troubled with the mail again.'

There was a barely audible chuckle and someone muttered under their breath, 'Nigel's met his match!'

Liz was glad of the backlog of work. The tedium of entering invoices in the purchase ledger was a good excuse to keep her head down and no-one interrupted except Mr Nigel, checking her progress, drumming his fingers impatiently as usual.

* * *

The knocking-off horn went at noon and the office and yard emptied as everyone went home for their dinner, the main meal of the day. The girls in the office left five minutes before the yard.

Liz always walked home with Sylvia McDonald, her best friend and next-door neighbour. Sylvia, plump and pretty, was the eldest of Olive McDonald's three girls.

'It's a shame you weren't made secretary, but you don't really have enough experience, I suppose,' Sylvia remarked. 'Nippy Nigel wanted you promoted, but you'd never have been fully the secretary. He'd already taken over some of the jobs, like the mail, for instance. He's really enjoyed himself these last few weeks, seeing everything first.'

Liz had to acknowledge that without Nippy Nigel's help she'd never have managed the secretary's position for the past seven weeks.

'You would have been nothing but a glorified typist,' Sylvia went on. 'He'd have had you under his thumb.'

'Maybe so,' Liz agreed. 'But though he may be pernickety, he still backed me. And the extra salary would have been a boon.'

The girls continued on their way in silence until they heard someone come running behind them, then Keith Watson reached them, still in his dungarees.

'She didn't get the job!' Sylvia answered his question before he asked, and enjoyed telling of the able Mrs Martin's surprise arrival.

As they reached Dumbarton Road, she turned to them.

'I must pop into Greg's and see what we're doing tonight,' and she hurried across the road to the butcher's where her boyfriend, Greg Scott, was the charge-hand.

Liz and Keith were waiting at the kerb to cross when he dropped his bombshell.

'I'm leaving Burnham's. I've got a berth as third engineer on the Turnbull. She sails on Sunday morning from Yorkhill Quay.'

'Oh no . . . ' It was out before Liz

could stop herself. 'I mean . . . that'll be nice for you,' she finished lamely. The prospect of Keith going out of her life, on top of the job disappointment, made this a bleak day.

'It'll be a longish trip going to Canada then America and down through the Panama Canal into the Pacific,' he explained, then asked, 'Will you write to me?'

'Oh yes. If you want me to . . . ' Liz nodded quickly. 'When did you decide this?'

'It's a long story. Come to the pictures with me tonight and I'll explain.'

'I'll enjoy that,' Liz murmured as he put his hand under her elbow and led her safely across the road.

She was cautiously elated. She and Keith had often gone to the pictures with friends but this was the first time he had asked her on her own and the significance was not lost on her. After all, young Glasgow engineers often went to sea when they wanted to save up to get married . . .

As they walked up the slope of Yarrowholm Street, her father joined them, and it was obvious that he knew she'd not been promoted.

The doors of the flats stood open for the men to go straight in and save precious minutes. Keith Watson stopped on his threshold on the second floor.

'I'll come up about seven,' he murmured to Liz and went in, dourly followed by his father.

Robbie Johnstone shook his head as he entered the flat.

'Eddie Watson used to be a pleasant fellow, but now he doesn't give anyone the time of day,' he commented to his wife, as she stood ready to ladle out the soup

Esther nodded and sighed.

'I don't know how his wife puts up with him. No wonder the two girls got married as soon as they could to get away. And now Keith's got himself a berth to Canada so he'll be off, too.'

Andrew came eagerly from the

bedroom when he heard Liz's footsteps, but his face fell when his sister shook her head.

'I'm afraid we won't be having that meal at the Malmaison this week,' she told him sadly.

Andrew smiled. 'No matter. We'll do it with my first doctor's salary.'

'How's the studying?' she asked.

'OK. I just hope what I'm doing comes up in the exam — or else.' He drew a finger across his throat.

Liz nodded. Re-sits were something he worked very hard to avoid, aware as he was of the strain that his studies put on the family's finances.

Esther gave her daughter a quick sympathetic hug.

'I'm sorry you didn't get the promotion. You wanted it so badly, too.'

'Thanks, Mum. You were right, though — I really don't have enough experience yet.' Liz tried to smile. 'Our new neighbour Mrs Martin's got the position.'

Esther listened as Liz described her morning, but the conversation was cut short by the twins, Jim and Frank, bursting into the kitchen, in high spirits as usual.

'Keith from downstairs has got third engineer on the Turnbull.'

The two young men crowded into the scullery to wash their hands. They envied Keith and longed for their apprenticeships to finish, desperate to travel further than Partick for cinemas and Clydebank Tech. for night classes.

Young Harry came in and took his seat at the table beside his sister.

'Sorry you didn't get the job, Liz. I've heard old Nippy Nigel is furious. He'd thought, with you as the M.D.'s secretary, he'd be in full charge of the office. But the big boss foiled him, and fixed himself up . . .'

'Get on with your soup. That's no way to talk,' Robbie Johnstone growled. He didn't approve of his youngest son calling Mr Alex Burnham 'the big boss', or the cashier 'Nippy Nigel', although everyone else in the yard called them that.

Esther frowned as she supped her soup. Robbie was so hard on the boy. It annoyed him that young Harry was always absorbed in a book. He didn't mind the twins reading for their night school, or Andrew for university, or Liz reading to improve her office skills, but to read books for pleasure, as young Harry did, irritated him, especially as the lad admitted his ambition was to be a newspaper reporter.

To Robbie, people from Yarrowholm Street worked in the shipyards.

Esther had persuaded him to let Andrew take the medical bursary against his inclinations and it irked him that the others hadn't had the chance to go on at school. There was only room for one university student in this family and even then they'd had years of penny pinching.

Gradually the family rose from the table and Robbie and Esther were alone.

'Liz is disappointed she didn't get the promotion,' Esther murmured. 'She was hoping to start saving. After all, I got married at twenty-five — the age she is now.'

Robbie nodded. 'Has she mentioned that Keith Watson's asked her to the pictures tonight? It wouldn't surprise me if in another couple of years they might make a pair.'

The news wasn't unexpected to Esther. There had always been an unspoken affection between them.

'The Watsons are a strange kind of family . . . although Keith's a nice steady young man,' Esther mused, then described what had happened when the Canadian letter had arrived this morning.

'I've never seen Olive McDonald secretive in all the years I've known her, but she was that today,' she observed.

She repeated some of the place-names she'd heard her neighbours mention after the postie had left, but they meant nothing to Robbie.

'Ach, don't worry about it. It's none of our business.'

He placed an unexpected kiss on her cheek, which made her smile immediately.

'Och, away you go! At this time of the day, too!' And, as usual, with no conscious effort he dispelled any lurking disquiet in her life.

★ ★ ★

After the dinner break, Liz returned to Burnham's and went back upstairs to the office, and her heart sank when she saw Will Robertson waiting at the door. She'd thought she'd done well to avoid him all morning and braced herself for his inevitable teasing.

'It's for the best, Liz,' he started, his voice unexpectedly kind, but she brushed past him.

'How considerate!' she retorted, her tone sarcastic.

'Don't run away,' he appealed, grabbing her arm. 'You know Nippy Nigel would have been in charge just as much as he is now,' he continued with an unaccustomed concern in his voice as he barred her way.

But she shrugged him off. She couldn't cope with his usual banter. Her disappointment was still a throbbing ache.

Angrily she pulled herself away and walked quickly to the cloakroom, and once inside she allowed a few frustrated tears to spill over, glad that the others weren't back yet.

Having grown up with four brothers helped Liz handle the normal office banter, but Will Robertson seemed to have singled her out to tease and had an odd knack for getting under her skin.

He had been unexpectedly brought in as chief assistant last year, and in Liz's eyes he was a stranger, too, for, unusually, none of his relatives worked in the yard and she didn't know anything about him away from Burnham's.

She splashed her eyes with cold water and, judging it to be safe now, went back to the office, but she groaned when she saw that he was still hovering.

'Actually Mr Burnham wants to see you in his office,' he told her.

'Thank you!' She nodded coolly, and curbed her curiosity over what it was about.

She went into the private office and gazed out at the shell of the latest ship, which men were swarming over. Red-hot rivets soared up from the braziers, being stopped expertly in flight by the catcher.

Liz loved to watch the three riveters swinging their hammers rhythmically in turn and was so engrossed that it was a jolt to find Mr Alex Burnham standing beside her — and to see the young woman with him.

'It's a pleasing display of precision, isn't it?' he agreed, following her gaze. 'Sadly it's a sight we'll lose when the new riveting gun is perfected.'

He stood for another moment gazing at the riveters, then he motioned the two young women into chairs in front of his desk.

'I've been very impressed with your work, Miss Johnstone, so I want you to be involved in the new costing department we're establishing. It will add to your workload, so you will have an assistant.'

His arm went out expansively towards the young woman whom Liz had recognised as June Martin, Eleanor Martin's pretty, fair-haired daughter.

June Martin surveyed the slim, neat girl beside her, but one glance from Liz's candid hazel eyes made her avert her gaze. They were so honest. She felt a surge of panic. How long would it take her to realise that behind their façade, she and her mother, now settled in the ground floor flat, were near paupers?

She was embarrassed that they had used every connection, no matter how flimsy, to get work. Her mother had met Mr Burnham years ago at a dinner party, and had used that to get an interview.

'Miss Johnstone, my cousin Nigel will

tell you of your extra duties, which will entail you working closely with Mr Robertson. He'll also advise you about your increase in salary.'

With a benevolent smile Mr Burnham stood up. The interview was finished.

★   ★   ★

Back in the outer office with her new assistant, Liz felt a little dazed with all that had happened since this morning, but she tried to disguise it when she saw the grin on Will Robertson's face.

Mrs Martin came over at once and addressed Liz.

'June has completed a business course, so she has the theory. I've no doubt you'll understand her lack of experience.'

Liz smiled and nodded, a little flattered at being acknowledged as a department head. She turned to June with a feeling of déjà-vu.

'Come with me and I'll show you

were to put your coat.'

In the cloakroom June stopped and faced her.

'You'd better know what you've been saddled with. I've never worked before. We've lived for the last few years in China, until my father died. Then we discovered he had no money and that we'd been living on credit for years.'

Anxiously Liz raised her hand to stop the flow. These were private, family matters which she felt she should not know. But June shook her head as if refusing the way out, and went relentlessly on.

'We went out by liner, first class, and came back as stewardesses — only because my mother hinted that my father had been a kind of missionary — which he wasn't.'

'Look, this is no business of mine,' Liz told June evenly. 'My only interest is in how you work.'

'I want to work, honestly' June insisted. 'So does my mother. It's been awful discovering we've been living a lie for years. My mother is very bitter about it. She's decided we'll pay back every penny, even if it means living among poor people for the rest of our lives.'

This took Liz aback, and she bent her head to stifle a smile, thinking of the tenants of Yarrowholm Street. In their three-apartment flats, with bathrooms and hot and cold water, they certainly didn't consider themselves 'poor people'!

The door burst open and Sylvia McDonald came rushing in.

'Have you heard that Keith's leaving?' she panted.

'Yes. He's going to sea. I'm seeing him tonight to hear all about it,' Liz answered, then went on smoothly, 'You won't have met my new assistant, Miss June Martin.'

As June extended her hand in greeting, Sylvia stared from one to the other, amazed, not sure which piece of information to follow up first.

Liz and Sylvia didn't get a chance to speak again until they met going home at the end of the day.

'So? Tell me all about it,' Sylvia demanded eagerly.

'Mr Burnham has decided . . . ' Liz started but Sylvia interrupted with an impatient exclamation.

'No, not the work! You and Keith.'

Liz paused for a moment. So much had happened today. To her surprise, Nippy Nigel seemed happy about the new system — some of it was his idea, as he pointed out. He was even mellow about Mr Burnham deciding to employ June Martin.

Best of all for her was the unexpected salary increase. She and Andrew would go to the Malmaison after all! But it had pushed her longed-for date with Keith to the back of her mind. Now she gave Sylvia brief details of their conversation at lunchtime.

'I thought he had something on his mind, that's why I left the two of you on your own,' Sylvia said with a heavy show of tact. 'And what are you going to wear?'

Liz shrugged. 'I haven't thought about it!'

Her afternoon supervising June Martin and being initiated into the new field of costing had left little opportunity to think of anything else.

The only snag in the new arrangement was the prospect of working with Will Robertson, but she kept that to herself.

'I suppose I'll wear my blue dress, with the navy edge-to-edge coat, and last year's good hat,' she murmured.

'Oh! He'll not be able to resist you,' Sylvia insisted loyally, and Liz laughed.

'I don't think Keith is so easily bowled over,' she warned, for she was mindful that his invitation had been casual and she wouldn't let herself build up her hopes. She'd been hurt already today by doing that.

'I'll see you before you go,' Sylvia said, as they separated to go into their respective top-floor flats.

The office stopped work fifteen minutes before the yard, and Liz was glad to have a few minutes alone with her mother to discuss her amazing day before the boys came in with all their banter. She was feeling light-hearted and looked forward to telling Keith about all the changes that had taken place in the office.

She went into the big room, where she slept in the set-in bed, long, red plush curtains disguising its presence. All her clothes hung in the cupboard, and she quickly made her selection for the evening.

⋆   ⋆   ⋆

Liz was ready and waiting at half past six, a dusting of powder and a slick of lipstick applied to her face, a feeling of excitement rising in her breast. She'd waited a long time for this evening. Her coat, hat and gloves lay ready on the couch, and when she looked at herself in the overmantel mirror, she was pleased at what she saw.

Quarter of an hour later the doorbell

rang and she ran to the front door, but it was Sylvia and her boyfriend Greg who stood on the doorstep.

'It's OK, we're not stopping,' Sylvia assured her. 'Greg's taking me for high tea, then on to the second house of the Empire. The Mill Brothers are top of the bill. I just wanted to see you in your glad rags.'

When they left, Liz went back into the big room to wait.

The minutes ticked by. She grew puzzled as Keith was five, then ten minutes late.

The twins put their heads round the door.

'Maybe he's changed his mind,' they teased, dodging the cushion she laughingly threw at them and running off downstairs to their evening classes.

However, as the grandfather clock in the hall chimed out quarter to eight, she began to feel annoyed.

Her mother came into the room.

'Maybe you should go down,' she suggested tentatively.

'Not on my first date!' Liz was definite.

The clock had just struck half past eight when the doorbell jangled, and Liz went to answer it. In the Kitchen Esther and Robbie sat either side of the fire, listening.

Liz opened the door, her face set and unsmiling. But then she gave a cry of alarm at the sight of Keith, still in his work clothes, staring wordlessly at her, his face pale and agitated.

'What's wrong? What's happened?' she asked hoarsely.

'Where Has She Gone?'

I just don't understand it. She's obviously planned it so carefully. She's taken all her clothes and other bits and pieces . . . '

Keith had come up to the Johnstones' flat, bewildered and heart-sick, to break the news to Liz and her parents that his mother had left home.

He looked appealingly to Robbie and Esther as if they could explain his mother's sudden disappearance, then lifted his hands and let them fall in a resigned gesture.

'Sorry — I've been over all this already.'

'I think you and Liz should go for a walk,' Robbie suggested quietly, noting how often the young man rubbed his hands anxiously together. 'It's a lovely evening and it'll be light for another hour or so.'

'Yes, maybe it'll help to clear my thoughts. They're a bit tangled,' Keith agreed.

He was silent as they walked in the late evening sunshine past the Grannie Well at Kingsway where, as usual, groups of racing cyclists in their club colours had made a stop. Some drank from the chained metal cup while others made running repairs to their machines or sat with their backs to the railings, resting before they resumed their journeys.

Liz didn't press Keith. He'd talked so much already tonight about his mother. The bleak three-line note she left to his father had wounded him:

'Edward,

'I'm leaving and I'm not coming back. You'll be happy for you've always said I hinder you. Got a job as a housekeeper. Good luck to Keith and the girls.

— Your wife, Jean.'

They walked up Anniesland Road, and branched off at Southbrae Drive, the lilac in the gardens of the fine stone villas perfuming the May evening. At a field of swaying spring flowers beneath Jordanhill College, they stopped. A friendly pony ambled over to them, and they petted it and fed it handfuls of the lush grass from the verge, as they had done when they were children.

Then they took a seat on the nearby bench and gazed down over the fields and houses to where the cranes lining the Clyde broke the skyline. Smoke from the house chimneys was starting to coil up into the cooling evening air.

'I'm sorry about your mother,' Liz said quietly. 'I don't think anyone knew she was going to leave.'

'I just don't understand it,' he said again. 'Tonight Mrs McDonald — over the landing from you — told Dad that she'd asked her about the kind of work she could get.'

'It must have been a terrible shock for him,' Liz murmured. It was the first time she had ever heard of Mr Watson making any approach to his neighbours in the tenement block.

'He often said she'd held him back, though I don't know why,' Keith told her. 'They eloped to Gretna when she was just sixteen and he was ten years older. Her parents put her out because I was on the way.'

At this candour the colour rose in her face. Such matters weren't spoken about so openly, and she felt uncomfortable in any case, for she didn't understand the situation in the Watson household. Her home was a happy place, and her parents loved one another dearly.

'But he's going to miss her — if he has to look after himself,' she commented. 'No more of the food he likes on the table, his clothes washed and pressed, or his boots cleaned for him every morning.'

Keith rubbed his forehead and sighed.

'Yet, it doesn't make sense. She never

said an unkind word about him . . . and she wouldn't let me or my sisters say anything, either. She seemed so content with her life . . . '

He frowned as if the whole matter was beyond his comprehension and Liz felt an overwhelming pity for him.

He took her hand in both of his and raised it to his lips, then released it.

'Sorry — first dates are supposed to be light-hearted affairs, not spent trying to make sense of a mother's disappearance. Not that I'm too worried. Mum's a practical woman. She's taken all her clothes, family photographs, and what jewellery she had. And she must have saved up some money — though I don't know how.'

After this he made an effort to change the subject, and talked about his new career at sea, starting on Sunday. He'd already discussed it with his father, and they'd agreed he should go as planned. After all, it was a good opportunity for a young and able lad, and he'd already handed in his notice at the shipyard.

Just after ten, they arrived back at the close. At the same moment the sound of laughter broke the silence of the gloaming as the twins, Jim and Frank, came up the slope of Yarrowholm Street.

There was no opportunity for her to let them know the date hadn't gone as planned, before they called out, 'What picture did you see? Any good?'

'I'll have to go,' Keith whispered under his breath. 'Will you explain to them?' and he turned, leaving her alone as he took the entry steps in great bounds.

At the mystified look on her brothers' faces, Liz wanted to smile for the first time this evening. But when she told them the news, they were horrified.

'Mrs Watson? No! She's not the type — even if Mr Watson's a bit eccentric,' Jim gasped.

'When we were wee and she was hanging out her washing in the green she always dried our tears, and bathed our skinned knees . . . ' Frank put in.

' — and she gave us big blackcurrant jam pieces oozing berries,' Jim interrupted.

They continued to reminisce in praise of Mrs Watson as they climbed the stairs and went into their home.

Esther nodded in agreement when she heard them.

'Ay, she loved having young ones around the house. She often took you pair to let me have a rest when you were toddlers and her own were at school.'

Esther remembered with a pang how kindly Jean Watson had been then. Indeed, it was only recently that she had become withdrawn and kept herself to herself.

Young Harry was at the kitchen table, as usual reading a book propped against the milk jug.

'Someone must know where she's gone,' he said, looking up from his book. 'She'd have had to walk with a

43

big suitcase to get a bus or a tram. Women at their sinks on Dumbarton Road opposite must have seen her,' he added, trying to gather the facts like the journalist he dreamed of becoming.

'Maybe she took a taxi,' his father offered dryly from his big chair at the fire. 'She could have watched for it and been in it in less than a minute. There'd be few about to notice, in mid-afternoon during a school time.'

As father and son debated how their neighbour could have left no trace of her departure, Esther suddenly thought back to this morning. She went over Jean Watson's visit to Olive McDonald next door and their furtive behaviour. Could Olive have had a hand in this?

A glance at the clock put the thought from her mind and she went briskly over to the kitchen bed recess and started turning down the covers.

'Go on now, your father and I want to get to bed.'

Robbie reached up to the curved brass pipe above the range and lowered the gas until the gas-mantle only glowed faintly, and the room was dim.

The twins took the hint, and Liz gathered up her things and followed them from the room after planting a kiss on her parents' cheeks.

It had been a momentous day in her life, too. She'd lost out on one promotion in the morning, but gained another in the afternoon. And in the evening she'd achieved her life-long ambition of going out with Keith Watson. Yet she felt strangely deflated as she got ready for bed.

The longed-for date had not turned out as she'd dreamed, but having her hand kissed had been an unexpectedly romantic gesture from the down-to-earth Keith.

Warmed by the memory, she pulled back the red plush curtains so that the big room might be lit by the street lamps below. The gas in this room was only lit on special occasions. Liz longed for the luxury of electric light like the McDonalds next door, but in this house, the stumbling block was the twenty pounds needed to install it.

★ ★ ★

She was in bed by the time she heard her brother Andrew's key in the lock, but he knocked softly on her door and she called him in.

He had been dispensing at the local surgery.

'Did you have a busy evening making up Dr Rankin's tonic bottles?' she asked, sitting up in bed with her arms wrapped round her knees.

'Ay — but I'm not complaining. It earns me pocket money. Dr Dugald says he remembers being an 'impecunious student'!'

Liz laughed at her brother's impersonation of the dour old doctor.

'He's given me great experience of general practice work, too. Some of the other students haven't even been inside a doctor's surgery other than as patients.' He paused for effect. 'And

46

. . . Dr Rankin's brother, Angus, came in tonight — and he's offered me a job as his assistant in Clydebank after I qualify. It won't pay much to start with, but enough to support myself.'

'Andrew! That's marvellous!' Liz cried.

'I can easily get to Clydebank by tram from here and I'll be able to give Mum something for my keep, too.'

As he chattered excitedly about his imminent finals and his new future, Liz hated to dampen his euphoria by telling him Keith's news, but when she did he wasn't that disconcerted, blaming Keith's father's attitude and commenting that he was surprised Mrs Watson had put up with him for so long.

After a few more minutes he got to his feet, and was about to open the door when he turned with elaborate casualness.

'Is one of the new neighbours in the bottom flat a pretty fair-haired girl?' he asked vaguely.

'Yes, June Martin.' Liz nodded. 'Actually she's my new assistant. She started in Burnham's this afternoon. Why?'

'Oh, I just wondered. I came bounding up the entry stairs and didn't notice her going up sedately in front and went crashing into her. But she assured me I didn't hurt her.'

He went on his way and Liz smiled. It wasn't often that Andrew noticed that a girl was pretty.

She lay down, half closing the red plush curtains of the set-in bed to blot out the flashes from the tram trolleys in the street below. They lit the room like lightning, making the shadowy three-piece suite and sideboard suddenly solid for an instant.

Sleep was soon in coming . . .

★ ★ ★

For the rest of the week Liz saw Keith for a little in the evenings, when he came up to give the Johnstones any news he had gleaned about his mother's disappearance.

· They were no nearer finding out where she'd gone, but he welcomed the opportunity to discuss how to help his father come to terms with her leaving. To everyone's amazement, the taciturn Eddie Watson was devastated.

By Saturday, though, the half-day in Burnham's office, Mrs Watson's disappearance was just another item of news, especially when Sylvia McDonald cornered Liz alone in the cloakroom.

'Greg asked me to marry him last night!' Sylvia announced in an excited whisper. 'Don't tell anyone though. I haven't told my sisters yet. He's meeting me at one, straight from work, and we're going to Partick for the ring.'

Liz hugged her delightedly.

'Oh, Sylvia, I'm so happy for you both! Your mother will be pleased, too.'

'We haven't told her yet either. You know what she's like! She'd insist on coming to help us choose the ring! But

Greg will speak to her later this afternoon.'

Then she appealed earnestly to Liz.

'You're not meeting Keith till half six, so could you be in our house when we get back? You're good at keeping her in her place, and I'm afraid of what Greg might say if she starts to plan our lives.'

Liz was flabbergasted, and suggested that the young couple might like to start as they mean to continue, with Greg and her mother having to work out some ground rules, but Sylvia wouldn't listen. She feared Greg would become annoyed with her cheerfully opinionated mother; he had his own very set ideas.

There was a knock at the door and June Martin interrupted nervously.

'Miss Johnstone, Mr Robertson is to take you down to the yard. You've to be shown the Loft.'

At this Liz and Sylvia stopped, astonished.

'The Loft! Are you sure?' Liz gasped.

'Yes, Mr Wingrave — I think he's what they call the chief loftsman? — sent a special invitation.'

'Golly!' Sylvia marvelled, her engagement forgotten for a moment. 'You'll be the first female ever to set foot in that hallowed place.'

Will Robertson led the way downstairs, through the time office, and the time clerks watched in surprise as he escorted her out into the clamour of the yard.

Many of the older tradesmen knew who she was and sketchily touched the skips of their oil-stained caps in gruff courtesy as she passed.

Liz saw her father and his two helpers straightening up from shaping a bow plate at the edge of their shed and gave a nervous little wave.

'I've only ever seen these places from the windows of the private rooms,' she murmured.

Will nodded. 'It all looks quite different from ground level, doesn't it?'

Mr Wingrave, who happened to live in the same tenement close as Liz, on the same landing as the Watsons, bowed courteously when she appeared at his door.

'Welcome to my kingdom, Miss Johnstone. Now, let me give you a guided tour.'

He pointed to the floor, and gave Liz a detailed description of what every marking meant and what the job of each man in the Loft entailed. He continued along the long, narrow building, talking all the while as he led the way.

Liz found all the technical details difficult to absorb and was relieved when he was called away for a few minutes.

'I can't take in half of what he's saying,' she confided to Will Robertson. 'Is it important that I should?'

'Not really,' Will assured her, 'but you're better to know roughly what goes on here.'

They both gave Mr Wingrave their full attention when he returned to escort them to a half-glazed office at the opposite end of the building.

'And this is my office. Come — we must celebrate this first visit of a young lady to the Loft,' he ended genially. 'We'll toast the occasion with a cup of coffee, shall we?'

Liz faltered, remembering Sylvia saying that coffee tasted awful.

'Is something wrong?' Will Robertson murmured.

'I've never drunk coffee,' she confessed, feeling embarrassed.

'Leave it to me,' he whispered as they climbed the few steps up to the door.

Outside in the yard the men used half-pint tea-cans with wire handles, but here bone china cups and saucers were laid out on a tray.

'And how do you like your coffee, Miss Johnstone?' Mr Wingrave enquired, holding up a pot with a long spout.

'Miss Johnstone will have white coffee, with sugar, and I'll have black,' Will Robertson said easily, ushering Liz to a chair.

She wondered at his ease in this

genteel environment. Tea was the drink for everyone she knew — but then, Will Robertson was a stranger.

He had never discussed his background, and hadn't served an apprenticeship here as the other men in the office had. He had come as an experienced cost clerk last year.

He always seemed very self-assured and his suits, she had noticed, were well tailored, while his shirts were never threadbare.

There had only ever been banter between them before, and that had mainly been one-sided — with teasing from him.

Cautiously she sipped the coffee, then relaxed when she found it quite pleasant.

Mr Wingrave sat down with them and chatted for a few minutes. Then he cleared his throat apologetically.

'Miss Johnstone, your parents are approached by everyone in our close in emergencies . . . isn't that so?'

'Well, my father keeps the keys for

turning off the water when there are burst pipes . . . ' she acknowledged, then hesitated, wondering what was coming.

Mr Wingrave gave a nervous cough.

'You have no doubt heard of the unfortunate incident concerning Mrs Watson, my neighbour across the landing. It happens that Miss Martha, my sister, happened to see Mrs Watson get into a taxi and heard her tell the driver to go to Partick Cross, from where she would direct him.'

Liz sat waiting for him to explain further, but he seemed to think he had said enough, and it was Will Robertson who got the man's meaning.

'And you think it would be helpful if Miss Johnstone's parents were told of this?'

'Exactly,' Mr Wingrave agreed with some relief. 'It is a rather delicate situation for me, since Mr Watson is one of my shipwrights.'

Finally Liz realised what was expected of her.

'I'll mention it to them,' she said, and put her cup and saucer on the desk, realising now why she had been asked up here.

Mr Wingrave hastened to assure her that he had been anxious to let her see the Loft in her new capacity as cost clerk. Then, as he showed her through to the outer office, he continued, 'I trust you welcome this opportunity to further your career. You have a professional, no-nonsense approach, and it was accepted that at twenty-five you're past the usual age for marriage. Our Mr Nigel specially insisted that we give you the chance.'

Instead of feeling encouraged by this Liz felt depressed as she walked back to the office with Will Robertson. She was hurt to discover that her employers had openly discussed her being past marriageable age — and obviously considered her plain into the bargain.

'Hmmm! I don't entirely agree with that,' Will grunted, picking up on her thoughts. 'With a little encouragement there are several men here who would jump at the chance to ask you out. And he obviously doesn't know you were out walking with a young man from the engine shop on Monday evening.'

'How do you know that?' she gasped.

He shrugged. 'I saw you. My grandparents live in Southbrae Drive. It's a favourite walk for courting couples.'

She paused, then explained quietly, 'It was Keith's mother who left home. He's a neighbour and was at his wits' end trying to make sense of it.'

'Sounds as if she was heading for one of the big houses in Hyndland — ' he mused ' — or else the Broomielaw for a banana boat to the Caribbean!'

Liz glared at him. He had almost seemed likable until his mention of a banana boat which reminded her of the delight he took in teasing her.

Liz was glad to get back to her desk, where June Martin looked up from entering figures in a ledger.

'Am I doing this correctly?' she

whispered, glancing cautiously to the open door of Mr Nigel's room.

Liz examined her work and nodded.

'The main thing is to make your figures neat, so fours and sevens can't be confused.'

June nodded miserably.

'Mr Nigel's got me so scared I'm almost afraid to put pen and ink to the ledgers.'

'He does go on a bit — that's why he's known as 'Nippy Nigel'!' Liz told her with a smile. 'But he's very thorough, and the department has a good name.'

Liz remembered how terrified she herself had been of him when she'd first started with the books, yet hadn't he turned out to be very loyal to her, pressing for this promotion for her when she had missed out on the secretary's position?

As it happened, after almost a week of watching Mrs Martin as secretary, Liz was honest enough to admit June's mother was very good at her job

— certainly better than she herself would have been.

As they finished checking the figures June looked up and asked in a little rush, 'Do you have a brother, Andrew? I . . . I think I met him on the stairs one evening . . . '

'Oh yes, I hear he almost bowled you over! He was a bit excited that night — he'd just been promised a position as assistant to a doctor in Clydebank after he graduates in a month's time — we hope!'

'He was most charming,' June said with a smile, and bent back to her books.

Liz didn't give the implications of June's interest much thought as she carried on working on the ledgers. Instead her thoughts wandered to Will Robertson's remarks about her being more encouraging to the young men she knew.

Perhaps if she could say with ease, as June had, that a young man was 'charming', it might be easier — but she didn't have that gift, and was more inclined to take refuge behind her sharp tongue.

Compared to June and her mother she was gauche and unsophisticated. She hadn't the first idea how to react properly to compliments when they came.

She smiled wryly to herself, aware that it was only since they had come into the office that she had realised this was a problem. She had had her eyes opened by their stylish and sophisticated ways.

Friends And Neighbours

That evening when Esther Johnstone glanced at the clock up on the kitchen mantelpiece, the hands were nearing 7.30 p.m.

She'd wanted to hear from Liz all about how Olive McDonald had taken her daughter's engagement, but for the last hour Keith had talked non-stop about Miss Wingrave seeing his mother leave. Now he was exploring the possibility of her being a housekeeper in a West End mansion.

Robbie shook his head at this.

'I doubt it. Someone would have found out by now, and she'd have got word to you or your sisters, to put your minds at ease — it's only a few miles up the road.'

Keith, sitting forward on one of the kitchen chairs, his head down, nodded slowly.

Esther was so weary of this constant inquest into his mother's leaving home. They'd had it every night this week and were no further forward.

It annoyed her, too, that he seemed oblivious to Liz, dressed up in her best clothes, waiting patiently in the background for him to take her out.

'Don't you think, Keith, that you and Liz should go if you want to catch the second house of the pictures?' she said, and there was such exasperation in her voice that Robbie jerked round to her, startled by her tone.

Keith stood up awkwardly.

'Yes, I suppose we've covered all eventualities.'

'Twenty times over!' Esther wanted to say, but the rules of hospitality made her bite her tongue as she escorted the two young people to the door and wished them a pleasant evening.

When she returned, Robbie looked at her questioningly, but she avoided his eye as she sat down opposite him and lifted the basket of socks and darning wool from the hearth on to her knee.

In truth, she was a little ashamed of her bluntness, but she'd had enough.

'The lad's upset by his mother's action and his father's sense of loss,' Robbie said mildly.

'Very commendable!' Esther sniffed. 'And I hope he gives Liz a good night out for supporting him in his time of trial. Though I've the feeling he doesn't notice — he's the type who just takes it for granted.'

Robbie stayed quiet. By the looks of things Esther's feathers had been ruffled.

'And the cheek of Eddie Watson expecting his two daughters to leave their husbands to come and look after him,' she fumed as she pushed the wooden mushroom vigorously up a thick working sock, her lips pursed at the thought. 'Even if they wanted to help, how could they afford the fares back and forward to Glasgow from Ayrshire?'

The Watsons' daughters had met

their respective husbands at haymaking time at the farm up the hill a few years ago.

It had caused some scandal, too, when the two girls had married in the registry office because Eddie Watson had refused to finance the usual small wedding celebrations. He'd been affronted because they were marrying 'mere farm workers'.

Robbie put on his jacket.

'I'm making up the pairs for the club championships tonight. I shouldn't be too long.'

Esther nodded. She didn't grudge him his Saturday evenings spent down at the bowling club. Tea was the strongest thing on offer down there.

Not like Eddie Watson and his ex-serviceman's club — she'd often seen him trying to hide his unsteadiness as he came home to his wife. And now he was supposedly grief-stricken! She pursed her lips, reflecting that she'd always said the Watsons were a strange family.

She continued to darn the socks with a thoughtful frown creasing her forehead.

She wanted Liz to have as happy a courtship as she'd had. She remembered clearly when she'd first met Robbie. It had been her night off from scullery work in the big house at Skelmorlie.

He'd danced every reel, jig and waltz with her, then walked her home to the servant's entry. Then he'd waited for her each evening until she'd finished work. The cook had ridiculed her and said he wouldn't write as he promised — but he had, and she still had the letters tied up with ribbon.

As she took a moment to check her handiwork she wondered if she was foolish to want someone who would give Liz that kind of romance and dedication. She doubted Keith Watson could . . .

Just then, the doorbell jangled and Esther brightened. It would be Olive McDonald from next door. She often looked in for a chat when she heard

Robbie going out to the bowling.

Esther hurried to the door, looking forward to hearing all about Sylvia's engagement and wedding plans.

However, her heart sank when she saw her neighbour dabbing her eyes with a handkerchief.

'Oh, Mrs Johnstone! Esther! Sylvia and Greg Scott are engaged. Got the ring and everything . . . and . . . oh! It's a judgement on me!' Olive choked.

Esther groaned inwardly. Tonight she would have enjoyed Olive's cheery gossip, but it seemed, once again, she was fated to listen to a story of misery.

'Come on in, Olive,' she said, hiding her feeling of resignation. 'The kettle's on the hob. Tell me all about it over a cup of tea.'

★ ★ ★

Robbie came up the stairs whistling, glad to be out of the chill, gusting rain, which was so unseasonable for the end of May. He was pleased, too, that the

66

bowling club meeting had been short. Now he was looking forward to Esther's spiced fruit pie for supper.

However, as he stepped over the threshold, sounds of loud sobbing came from the kitchen and he groaned. It sounded like Olive McDonald from next door. Never one for the happy medium, she was either highly elated or in the depths.

'Oh, there's your husband back,' Olive wailed to Esther. 'I'll just go. You'll remember though. Not a word to him — ' she pointed a forefinger downwards ' — him downstairs . . . that Eddie Watson . . . about Jean's suitcase, or the letters. I swore on oath I wouldn't tell him.' And Olive left, sniffing and sighing.

'What was all that about?' Robbie asked when Esther returned from seeing her out.

Esther gave a long sigh.

'It seems that Olive was taking in Jean Watson's letters, from her brother in Canada. There was money in the one that came on the day she left.' She sat down opposite him. 'And Jean's suitcase was in Olive's flat too — she'd packed it over the past week or so, one item at a time.'

'So Olive helped Jean Watson to disappear? Does she know where she's gone?' Robbie asked.

'She never said, and I didn't ask.' Esther gave another sigh. 'The truth is, Olive's very upset. Sylvia and Greg Scott got engaged this afternoon, and young Greg's made it clear that she's not to meddle in their lives. Now Olive is cut to the heart. She thinks it's a judgement on her for secretly helping Jean Watson to get away.'

Robbie was mystified by the woman's logic.

'But Sylvia's engagement and Jean Watson's leaving aren't connected!' he protested.

Esther shrugged. 'I know that — but Olive is superstitious . . . ' Just then, the doorbell jangled again and they looked at one another, puzzled. Visitors usually came earlier than this.

'You go,' Esther told her husband. 'If it's Olive back again, you deal with her,' she appealed, ignoring his horrified expression.

Alone for a moment, Esther stared into the flames licking round the coals in the grate, trying to make sense of Jean Watson's sudden departure — but she remained mystified.

Hearing a woman's voice at the front door caught her interest and moments later Robbie brought in Eleanor Martin.

'Oh, your kitchen is so comfortable and cosy,' she exclaimed, admiring the armchairs by the fire, the cushion covers made with colourful crocheted squares, the table spread with a green chenille cloth with a potted, broadleafed aspidistra in the middle, but most of all the warm fire in the shining grate of the cooking range.

'I've come uninvited like this to ask your help,' she admitted and came straight to the point. 'How is this type of fire kindled?'

Esther was startled. It seemed a strange request.

'And to ask about repairing the gas mantle. Ours is broken,' Eleanor continued apologetically, relieved to have unburdened herself.

'You'll need to buy a new one at Renton's Hardware Store,' Esther explained, then asked, 'Why won't the fire light?'

Eleanor Martin looked down at her long, red-tipped nails, and admitted that she hadn't managed to get it lit since their arrival.

'You've had no fire?' Esther was astounded. 'Then — you've had no hot water either?'

Shamefaced, Eleanor nodded, and saw the questioning look the Johnstones exchanged. She realised then that what she sought was so simple to them that they were puzzled.

'I was brought up in a Surrey vicarage,' she began in explanation. 'The housekeeping skills my mother taught me are very different from those required for a tenement flat.' She didn't mention the cook, the maid and the daily help who had done the household chores.

'I can earn a living now because my mother insisted I take a business course. You see, as a vicar's wife I'd have found it helpful, and, of course, she thought I might marry a clergyman. But I married my first boss when I was nineteen.'

She told them how June had been born a year later, how they had then lived all over the world, and had been in China running an expatriate British Club when her husband had died suddenly. His affairs had been in disarray, and there had been no money left when the bills were paid.

'So now we have to support ourselves. We were glad to rent the flat downstairs with some basic furniture, but I'm hoping ours will arrive in a week or two and we can live in some comfort again.'

'You're not using old Jock Hoskins' things!' Esther gasped.

When she and Robbie had come to Yarrowholm Street twenty-six years ago, the old soldier had already been living there and he'd never decorated or repaired anything since.

Eleanor nodded. 'We threw out such piles of old newspapers when we took over! And we've washed the curtains and scrubbed everything we can think of.'

'The flues in the range are probably full of soot from Jock's time,' Robbie commented ruefully.

Just then Andrew appeared from the bedroom, where he'd been studying. He was introduced to the new neighbour, and his mother explained the Martins' plight.

'Dad and I could go down to have a look at the range,' he immediately offered, looking to his father before noticing that Robbie was comfortably settled in his chair with his slippers on.

'It only needs one to get a fire going. You go, Andrew,' Esther urged. 'And, Mrs Martin, you'll stay and have a bit of supper with us, won't you?' she insisted.

She was horrified that the two women had been living in such discomfort. True, their frugal shopping had surprised the neighbours, but now Esther understood and respected their thrift.

'How kind of you.' Eleanor was touched by their hospitality. 'June's in, and I think she's already met you, Andrew.'

He nodded, and went out taking tools and a spare gas mantle with him.

Eleanor's eyes grew round as Esther set out fine china, then plates of scones, squares of spiced fruit pie, date loaf, butter and jam.

'I haven't seen such a spread for years,' she murmured.

* * *

It was dark and gloomy as Andrew went downstairs to the Martins' flat. The lamp leerie hadn't been to turn on the gas lamps in the close yet, so there was only the late brightness of the evening sky which barely reached the door behind the banister.

'Who is it?' a girl's muffled voice asked when he knocked.

'Andrew Johnstone from upstairs!'

He listened in disbelief as bolts were pulled, chains removed and the door key was turned. No-one in Yarrowholm Street barricaded themselves in like this!

The door opened a few inches, and June Martin's anxious, pretty face, lit by the candle in her hand, peered round. Then she smiled and flung the door wide.

'Oh, it's you! Sorry for being so suspicious but living out East does that to you.'

'I've come to see to your kitchen fire,' Andrew explained as he followed her to the kitchen.

First he replaced the gas mantle, and in moments light flooded the room.

'Oh, thank you,' she breathed gratefully. 'No light on a grey evening like this was the last straw.'

Andrew glanced round the dismal kitchen but hid his surprise at the state of it as he started cleaning out the half-burnt coals and sticks in the grate, evidence of their previous futile attempts to light the fire. Then he showed her how to clean out the soot and ash from the flues.

'Thank you so much,' she said, sincerely grateful. 'We're truly in your family's debt. Your sister Liz has been so kind in the office and now you've given up your time for us.'

'It's no trouble. I've had my head in my books all day, so I'm glad of the break — my medical finals are in a couple of weeks, you see.'

He stood back with a satisfied nod as the firewood took light, and before many minutes had passed he was telling her about life at university while June told him about some of their experiences from their travels.

Soon the coals were glowing redly and there were flames dancing in the fireplace.

'It's so simple now that I've seen you do it,' June marvelled, as he filled the coal scuttle from the bunker under the window. 'The old gentleman who lived here didn't seem to worry about furniture,' she went on, 'but his store cupboards were well stocked — and that coal store.'

They had been living on old Jock's tinned food, only buying milk and bread when necessary.

'Mother and I are determined never to get into debt. It was so awful finding my father owed money to everyone. That's why Mummy decided we should start afresh in Scotland. We've already managed to save enough to get our furniture out of store next week.'

Her candour surprised Andrew, and he wondered how her sophisticated mother would feel about the details of their life being revealed.

He insisted that June should come upstairs for supper with the family.

'You can't sit down here alone while the rest of us are tucking into my mother's Saturday supper!'

Blushing, she gave in, but apologised profusely for intruding as she took her place beside her mother at the Johnstones' supper table.

'We've got a fire blazing in a shining grate!' she announced excitedly.

'Yes — after pails of ashes and soot went out to the midden,' Andrew added, then gave a mischievous wink. 'Now June knows how to clean out the range and the flues, and that Friday night is when folks Zebo the grate.'

'Use a pair of old gloves, dear, to protect your hands,' Esther advised above the laughter.

June giggled self-consciously.

'We must seem so foolish, knowing none of these things. Still, if you ever decide to go to China I'll be able to show you how to get a stove going there — or to Germany, where they have tiled ones in the corner of the room.'

The two women entertained the Johnstone family with more tales of their travels until Liz and Keith returned just before ten. Liz had invited Keith in for Saturday night supper on his last night at home. It was one of the reasons they'd returned early, and they were surprised to hear laughter and merry voices coming from the kitchen.

'No, I won't bother now, thanks,' Keith said stiffly when Liz urged him to stay. 'It sounds as if your parents are entertaining. I'll just go down and keep my father company. He's missing my mother dreadfully. I'd be a bit of a wet-blanket going in when everyone is so light-hearted,' he finished, and Liz nodded dully. It was a fitting end to an ill-starred evening.

The cinema they'd gone to had been full, so they'd walked round the town in the rain looking for another film to see. However, the situation had been the same at every picture house they'd tried, and so they'd eventually come home.

'You will write to me, won't you, Liz?' Keith dug his hand into his inside pocket and brought out an envelope.

'Here are the shipping agents' addresses for the ports we'll be putting into. Let me know how my father is coping.'

Liz took the envelope and nodded, her heart full of disappointment. It seemed that all her life she'd longed to be taken out by Keith, but she had never dreamed it would be so dull. She had carried a torch for him for so long, and now she wondered if perhaps there was something lacking in herself?

'Sorry, this isn't how I planned ... wanted ... looked forward to us ... ' He floundered, trying to find words to explain his dashed hopes. Then he took her by the shoulders. 'Liz, I'll see you when I get back in a few months. It will be better for us then.'

He planted a clumsy kiss on her cheek, and was running downstairs to his own home before she could reply.

Liz closed the door softly and realised from the continued jollity in the kitchen that no-one knew she was home. She went quietly to the big room, and stood at the oriel window looking down to the wet roads and pavements under the street lights. Only an occasional tram passed beneath her as couples, cosily arm in arm, walked home under umbrellas.

A gust of laughter came from the kitchen, bringing tears to her eyes. She felt so alone, and somehow cheated of something very precious.

'I thought I heard you come in.' Esther's voice came behind her, but as her eyes searched Liz's face she decided not to comment on the evidence of recent tears.

'I've just been seeing the new neighbours out. What good company Eleanor and June Martin are! We haven't laughed so much in ages.' She chatted on, all the while carefully watching Liz.

'Whatever happened at Sylvia's engagement?' she enquired lightly. 'I had Olive McDonald over earlier and I couldn't get anything much from her, other than that she's not pleased.'

It took Liz a moment to focus on their next-door-neighbours, and Sylvia and Greg's engagement announcement.

'Mrs McDonald was over the moon to start with, then, as usual, she started making plans for them and taking over. Greg disagreed with her ideas and she didn't like it, then one word led to another . . . ' Liz shrugged, leaving her mother to picture the scene of domestic strife across the landing.

'And Fiona McDonald's not too happy either,' Esther reflected. 'It looks like our Andrew's quite taken with June Martin from downstairs. And I must say, she's a lovely girl.'

Liz raised an eyebrow. Nothing escaped her mother. Fiona, the middle McDonald daughter, had made no bones about wanting Andrew and she hoped that once he was finished studying they would make a pair.

'June's worked hard to learn the books at Burnham's,' Liz murmured, but she knew her mother was waiting for her to explain being home so early, and without Keith.

'You were right — all the picture houses were full.' She tried to sound normal as she continued, 'So I brought him back here. I thought he'd enjoy one of your Saturday suppers before he went to sea. But we could hear you had visitors and he — ' Liz stopped, the sense of disappointment overpowering her, and her voice cracked. She turned away, trying to regain her composure.

Esther frowned. 'I always said the Watsons were a strange family.'

First Steps For Harry

Burnham's office was busy for the next week, and nobody noticed that Liz was quieter than usual. Besides, Sylvia's engagement was the main topic of conversation among the female staff.

'Greg's decided we'll look out for a room and kitchen to rent, then set the date for the wedding,' Sylvia announced confidently to the girls.

But Liz, who had been at the engagement announcement, knew things were more complicated than that. Sylvia's mother was not a happy woman, so there would be difficulties ahead.

As the days went by, Liz had to have a quiet word with Sylvia about the amount of time she was spending away from her drawing board. As often as not her two sisters, Fiona and Lindsey, were with her, discussing wedding plans in the cloakroom.

On Friday afternoon Mr Nigel came out and stood by her desk, staring pointedly at the three empty drawing-boards under the window.

'Miss Johnstone, come into my office, and ask Mrs Martin if she would come, too. You are the senior ladies and we must discuss this.'

Liz's heart sank. If she hadn't been so preoccupied, she would probably have warned Sylvia more seriously that this was bound to happen.

When they went into his office, Mr Nigel was frowning as he took up his usual position, half sitting on the edge of his high stool. Liz knew it was the only concession he made to his artificial limb. He had lost his right leg below the knee, during the Great War at the battle of the Somme.

'The chief draughtsman has asked me to investigate why the tracers are so often away from their boards when his men are waiting for their work. He assumes that since they are in my office it's my responsibility.'

He looked at them both, waiting for their reaction.

After a moment's reflection Eleanor Martin voiced her thoughts.

'I agree that Sylvia is exhausting everyone's goodwill. But isn't the chief draughtsman passing the buck expecting you to reprimand his staff? They may be in your office but they're hardly your department, are they? The matter would be resolved if the tracers were relocated in the drawing office, under the eye of the chief draughtsman.'

Liz nodded her agreement. It was a sensible solution.

Eleanor continued, outlining a plan which involved better use of the office space.

However, Mr Nigel was not entirely convinced about having the lady tracers in with the male drawing office staff.

'Previously, it was not thought proper for young ladies to be in such a male environment as the drawing office.'

'But men and women work side by side in the commercial office,' Liz pointed out.

Mr Nigel remained silent for a moment, then straightened up. He'd kept his military neatness, his suit was well tailored, his shirt pristine white, the stiff white collar exactly in position.

'Thank you, ladies — I'm grateful for your help.'

He opened the door and politely let them both walk out in front of him, then went purposefully to Mr Burnham's office.

As usual, the Managing Director made a swift decision. The tracers' drawing boards were being dismantled when Sylvia and her sisters emerged from the cloakroom

'It has been decided that from now on you will work from the drawing office,' the Managing Director told them smoothly. 'My secretary, Mrs Martin, needs more space.'

On Saturday morning the warmth of the sun was pleasant as Liz and Sylvia walked to Burnham's.

'Did you go and see Keith off on Sunday?' Sylvia asked.

'No. He said his goodbyes on Saturday evening. But he asked me to be sure to write.'

Liz hoped this would satisfy Sylvia. It was still too painful to discuss.

'And have you written?' Sylvia pressed.

Liz nodded. 'I've got one to send off tonight.'

She had been prepared to write every day, but somehow the fiasco of their two dates had restrained her.

This seemed to satisfy Sylvia, and her sense of hurt pride over the office move bubbled to the surface.

'Why was it suddenly decided to put us into the drawing office?' she burst out. 'Was that new secretary behind it? Not that I'm worried, for it's a more sensible arrangement.'

Liz looked straight at her friend, and spoke bluntly.

'Word came from the yard that drawings weren't arriving on time, and men on piece-work aren't interested in wedding arrangements.'

Sylvia giggled.

'I suppose I was overdoing it,' she conceded. 'But you'll understand how it is when you and Keith get engaged.'

Liz turned away quickly. She wondered if that would ever happen, and even if it did — would it bring the kind of contentment her parents had enjoyed in their marriage?

She took some comfort from the fact that Keith had shared her disappointment when their dates had gone so badly wrong and wondered if they might have been different if he hadn't been so preoccupied with his mother's disappearance.

★ ★ ★

Later that morning Will Robertson called to her.

'Come on, Liz! Let's check on a few jobs.'

She pretended not to notice his use of her Christian name, which was frowned on during office hours.

They donned brown linen warehouse coats and went down to the clamour of the yard again.

She concentrated hard as it was essential that no tradesman's time was left out of their calculations.

The costing methods Burnham's used were the same as when the chief clerk had started fifty years before. Now he was due to retire at the Glasgow Fair, and Will would be promoted. He was eager to introduce more modern costing procedures when he took over.

They gazed at the towering mass of the ship under construction. Men were clambering all over it, and the noise of riveters and platers hammering was nearly deafening.

'The last time I stood here, there was grass growing up from the concrete,' Liz remarked, almost to herself.

'I thought you'd never been down in the yard before last week?' he queried.

'It didn't count. It was ten years ago, when I first started in Burnham's. The yard wasn't like this when my father brought me. It had just reopened after five years.'

Liz stopped, surprised at how easy it had been to start a conversation with Will Robertson. She was wary of his teasing, but since working with him she'd come to admire his quick brain.

'Was that when Mr Burnham first took in orders to build land boilers and river boats?' he asked.

Liz nodded, remembering her father's pride that he'd kept every piece of machinery in working order during the closure. And he'd impressed on her how fortunate she was to become the office girl, frightened though she was by the strict regime.

'I remember,' she mused, 'being

surprised at how narrow the river was, and wondering how huge ships could be launched into it.'

'I suppose your father said, 'Glasgow made the Clyde, and the Clyde made Glasgow'.' Will grinned. It was an anthem all the shipyard workers repeated with pride.

'The channel had to be specially widened and deepened past John Brown's yard for the Queen Mary launching last September,' Will remarked.

Liz remembered that afternoon. They'd listened to the commentary on Mr Burnham's radio, marvelling at the descriptions of the crowds who'd come in the pouring rain to see the great liner being launched in Clydebank by Queen Mary herself.

Liz glanced over to the platers' shed, and saw the tall figure of Mr Wingrave, the chief loftsman, with her father. They were both engrossed in a newspaper which they were holding open between them.

Will nodded over. 'Your father's

finding something interesting in Mr Wingrave's paper. Is Henry Lavelle Johnstone a relative of yours?' he asked.

'That's my youngest brother's name. Why?'

Will pulled out a folded newspaper from his pocket, and handed it to her.

'Could he have written this piece about the early shipyards on the Clyde? It's interesting,' he went on. 'Well researched, too. Told me plenty of things I didn't know.'

Liz felt a pang of foreboding as her eyes scanned the article. There would be trouble ahead at home if Harry had written this.

'It could be Harry . . . ' she conceded with a frown.

'We'll ask him when we go through the time-office,' Will said, sounding delighted, but Liz shot him a warning look.

'Please, keep it quiet for now,' she pleaded, and explained her father's unease over Harry's ambitions to write.

'That's a short-sighted attitude,' Will commented, and indicated the paper. 'If this *is* your brother's work, he's got real talent. He could make a good career with newspapers.'

Privately Liz agreed, but she had to speak to Harry, and when they returned through the time-office she searched anxiously for a sight of her young brother.

She was relieved to see him hanging up the numbered time-checks discs on their board.

'Harry, did you write an article for — ' she began.

'Is it in today? Have you got a copy?' His face was alight.

Will handed him the newspaper and Harry scanned the typescript with growing delight.

When he gave the paper back to Will, he looked to his sister, anxious appeal in his eyes.

'Liz, do you think Dad will be proud of me now?'

★　★　★

It was nearing Saturday lunchtime and Esther was just about to mash the potatoes when she remembered the newly-arrived letter for young Harry which was in her apron pocket.

She sighed as she slit it open. It was probably another rejection slip from an editor. They came regularly, but it didn't deter him from his dream of being a newspaper reporter.

Esther's face broke into a smile as she scanned the typewritten page and examined the two-guinea cheque attached to it. *The Clarion* had bought two articles!

Carefully she replaced the letter in the envelope and propped it up on the table for Harry to see when he came home.

She bit her lip. She was delighted for her son, but how would Robbie react? Her husband was so against Harry's interest in writing, yet already the boy had earned from it — and, what's more, he'd earned as much as Liz earned in a week in the shipyard offices.

Esther was thoughtful as she put the

potatoes to keep warm with the mince and went through to the big room to wait.

Liz was first home and came bursting into the room.

'Mum, Harry's had a —'

'I know.' Esther nodded. '*The Clarion* have taken two pieces from him — at a guinea a time!'

Liz gasped in disbelief then went on, 'I think Dad already knows about it,' and she described how she had seen him and Mr Wingrave engrossed in the newspaper.

'If a good paper like *The Clarion* accepts Harry's work, it's time your father was changing his mind about his disapproval,' Esther said decisively.

The boy's desire to be a newspaperman was one of the few things that divided his parents. To his father, a boy from Yarrowholm Street couldn't possibly earn a living from writing. He believed Harry should be content to follow a secure trade in the shipyard.

'I wonder if reporters have apprenticeships, and if Harry could get one?'

Esther reflected, planning the practicalities of her son's future.

At the sound of an extra set of footsteps coming up the last flight of stairs to the open front door, the two women exchanged an anxious glance. Robbie — and he had someone with him.

Robbie and Mr Wingrave came into the room and Esther smiled, nodding to the folded newspaper under Mr Wingrave's arm.

'So you know about Harry's piece — '

'Yes, quite remarkable from one so young,' Mr Wingrave interrupted enthusiastically. 'This is certain proof that the boy has good prospects as a journalist. I happen to be on friendly terms with the editor of The Clutha News and I'll have a word with him about the boy. There's no better place than a local paper for a keen lad to learn.'

Glancing cautiously at her husband, Esther saw his frown and knew he wasn't yet won over even though Mr Wingrave was respected by all the men in the yard and his opinion carried weight.

'It would be a dream come true for Harry,' she murmured, but loyalty to her husband prevented her revealing that their views were at odds over this.

When Harry came panting in he looked immediately at his father, but Robbie's face remained impassive and it was Mr Wingrave who excitedly shook his hand.

'A fine piece of writing, lad. Well researched, too. I never realised that John Brown's started in Sheffield way back in 1838, and made everything from cutlery to railway springs.'

'Yes, they've built ten ships on the Clyde for Cunard, including the Lusitania — isn't that right, Dad?'

Harry appealed eagerly to his father but Robbie merely nodded.

'I got lots of facts from just listening to my father,' Harry said quietly to Mr Wingrave, and Esther sensed his disappointment at his father's lack of support.

'The *Clarion* letter's in the kitchen. Go and see it,' she said quickly.

Harry came rushing back gleefully waving the cheque.

'Mum! Mum! I got two guineas!' He thrust the cheque into his mother's hand. 'You'll be able to buy Andrew a new suit for his graduation!'

Esther's heart filled at the boy's natural generosity as she passed the cheque to her husband, who stared at it in silent disbelief.

'Excellent! Excellent!' Mr Wingrave beamed.

Andrew and the twins, Jim and Frank, came in just then and as they were told Harry's news Robbie still stood quiet, astonished that nothing more than a few scribbled lines could have earned the boy so much.

'What do you think, Dad?' Harry asked anxiously.

'We'll wait and see what this editor fellow says,' he said. 'And you'd better keep this in case you need a suit yourself,' he added, abruptly handing back the cheque.

While he escorted Mr Wingrave out, Andrew went into the kitchen, where he saw the frustration on his youngest brother's face.

'I don't think Dad's very impressed,' Harry said gruffly. 'He'd be happier if I'd got an apprenticeship at the yard.'

Andrew put a consoling arm round the boy's shoulders.

'I know how you feel. I used to think he'd be prouder of me if I'd made the grade for Burnham's drawing office instead of winning a university bursary.'

'But why's he like that?' Harry asked.

Andrew shrugged ruefully.

'Dad's generation thinks getting a trade is the highest thing a working man can aspire to.'

'But he'll be proud of you when you're a doctor,' Harry said with more conviction than he felt.

'I certainly hope so! We'll soon see anyway — my finals start in a week's time.' Andrew sighed, then noticed the anxiety on Harry's face, and smiled reassuringly. 'Come on. Let's get our dinner before Frank and Jim start looking for seconds.'

★ ★ ★

During the next week or so in Burnham's office, the new costing department was set up in place of the tracers' drawing-boards. Liz had a desk there, too, beside Will Robertson, who was enjoying his new view of the street below.

'Wee Puggie's taking out that land boiler for Finland.' He beckoned the rest of the office staff over, who craned to see.

'In a month or so it'll be making electricity in Helsinki,' Will announced with some satisfaction.

June Martin was awed.

'That's remarkable!' she breathed.

'It is that,' Will agreed with some satisfaction. 'But Burnham's engineers are famous the world over for finding practical answers to unusual problems.'

They watched till the little engine chugged out of sight, then drifted back to their desks. Today, Liz and June were sitting side by side working on the accounts books.

It was Thursday, the last day of Andrew's medical exams, and Liz was finding it difficult to concentrate.

'What does Andrew sit today?' June had whispered every morning this week.

' . . . intensive medicine . . . surgery . . . orthopaedics . . . gynaecology . . . ' Liz murmured back on the appropriate day.

'Your family must be glad the end's in sight after all that sacrificing and saving,' June whispered at her side now.

'My mother's the one who's done most,' Liz admitted. 'She persuaded my father to let Andrew take the bursary, and somehow she's found the extra money he needed. Mind, it's not been easy for Andrew either, knowing he must succeed. But, all going well — ' Liz showed her crossed fingers ' — you and your mother must come up to the house tomorrow after the results. Mum's been secretly preparing for a little party and I expect all the neighbours in the close will come in,' she confided.

Liz had found the box at the foot of the kitchen press, with the cakes her mother usually only made at Christmas, as well as some fancy shop-bought biscuits. She hadn't mentioned it as her mother would never have admitted preparing for a celebration. It would be too much like tempting fate.

June shook her head ruefully.

'I feel so tense with this waiting — it must be unbearable for your family!'

'It was Andrew's second-year exams which were the worst for us.' Liz explained that that year's subjects had all had to be passed together. 'So if he'd faltered, his medical career would have stopped there. My father was especially worried for Andrew was too old by then for a shipyard apprenticeship. They always start at sixteen.'

'Thank goodness the results are out tomorrow. I can't stand this waiting!' June confided.

★ ★ ★

It was the middle of the Friday afternoon when the phone call came. 'I've done it! I've passed! I couldn't wait to tell you. Get word to Dad if you can. I'm heading straight home to tell Mum. See you at tea-time.'

Liz turned to face the office which had fallen silent.

'We've got a doctor in the house!' she announced, smiling through a blur of happy tears.

June joyfully threw her arms about Liz's neck and hugged her as the office erupted, drawing Mr Nigel and Mrs Martin out of his room where they had been working together. He shook Liz's hand, and there were tears in the eyes of the efficient secretary as she kissed Liz's cheek.

'Your family deserves this,' Eleanor

Martin said sincerely. 'You've all helped June and me so much.'

Even Mr Burnham, the managing director, came out to investigate what was going on.

'Excellent news! I'll get word to your father immediately.'

'That's grand,' Will Robertson murmured, and his sincerity surprised Liz. 'After years of study, it's wonderful to know you've earned the letters after your name.'

His comment set her wondering what he knew of years of study or putting letters after his name.

But then, Will Robertson was a mystery man in Burnham's. He had come fully-trained last year and no-one knew much about him or where he had come from.

That evening, a stream of friends and neighbours called in at the Johnstones' flat. Esther was so relieved and thankful at her son's success that she could do little more than sit and marvel with them.

The twins, with the help of Harry and Liz, made the tea and passed round the fancy cakes while their father and Andrew saw that all the men got a dram and the ladies a port or a glass of sherry.

Esther had been taken aback when Robbie had put a sherry in her hand with a knowing wink. It was only at New Year that he had such drink in the house, and she laughed. He had prepared in secret for this celebration, too!

Halfway through the evening, she caught Liz's sleeve as she passed.

'Liz, Keith's father's the only neighbour who hasn't come. Go down and invite him up.'

Liz frowned, for Mr Watson was a difficult man at the best of times.

Nevertheless, she went downstairs to the next landing and knocked at the door. Keith's father opened the door looking dishevelled; clearly he missed being properly looked after.

'Since my wife left I'm not good

company,' he said doubtfully when she explained why she had come.

'You might enjoy a change of scene,' Liz cajoled. 'All the neighbours are in.'

He paused, then shrugged.

'Oh well then . . . Come in and wait till I tidy myself up a bit.'

He walked away to the bedroom, and Liz went into the kitchen — and her heart leapt as she caught sight of an envelope on the mantelpiece. It was in Keith's handwriting, addressed to her!

She hesitated for a moment, then lifted it down, just as Mr Watson came into the kitchen, straightening his tie.

'Oh! You've got your letter? Keith gave it to another engineer in Canada whose ship was returning immediately to the Clyde. He brought it up with one for me the other day.'

Liz was annoyed at his delay in giving her the letter, but she made no remark, and led him upstairs to the party.

As soon as she could, though, she was back outside the door. Tonight it was the only place she would get peace.

She read Keith's letter quickly, then closed her eyes as she leaned back against the door. It wasn't a love-letter exactly, but she felt a thrill that Keith's first thoughts had been to get word of his safe arrival to her as quickly as possible.

She was even ready to overlook his father's tardiness about delivering the letter, but she couldn't help wondering how long it would have lain there, unopened, if she hadn't gone to invite him to the party.

As she was putting the letter back into the envelope, Mrs McDonald and her three daughters came out of the house. Liz wasn't surprised. They were uncomfortable near Mr Watson, who didn't know that Olive McDonald had helped his wife to leave home.

'Is that a letter from Keith?' Sylvia noticed immediately and Liz nodded with a bashful smile.

'It's just to be hoped he doesn't get his head turned by some flighty young thing on his travels,' Fiona McDonald commented sourly. 'Still, maybe by that time, Will Robertson will have taken Keith's place with you. He's trying hard enough!'

Liz was taken aback at this and had no idea how to respond.

At once, Sylvia apologised for her sister.

'Don't mind her. She's in a mood because she's got competition for your brother Andrew's attention. In fact, I'd say he's got a real soft spot for June Martin. After all, he spent hours helping her arrange their furniture the other weekend, didn't he?'

'The Martins have certainly brought a touch of sophistication to old Jock's flat,' Liz enthused.

Olive sniffed. 'Hmph! I think all that Chinese furniture and those rugs look stupid in a two-room and kitchen.'

Olive was put out to hear another flat being praised. Her home had been considered the best furnished and decorated in the close before Eleanor and June Martin had arrived.

'And imagine whitewashing the walls instead of putting up wallpaper,' Fiona said, backing her mother's criticism.

'That was done on purpose,' Lindsey, the youngest McDonald, disagreed sharply. 'The white walls set off the lovely colours in the carpets and rugs and the Chinese shades on their table lamps.'

'Yes, it's all very tasteful,' Sylvia agreed, then added thoughtfully, 'In fact, I think I'll ask Eleanor Martin's opinion when Greg and I start furnishing.'

Liz could hear the McDonalds still squabbling after the door opposite had closed behind them. The Martins had dented Olive's standing in the close and now she was voicing her displeasure that Sylvia should think of seeking Eleanor's advice rather than her own for her first home.

Liz sighed. This would be yet another cause of pre-wedding friction between Sylvia and her mother.

Her thoughts switched to Fiona's strange outburst. She had never considered that Keith might meet someone else. And as for Will Robertson and herself? It was preposterous!

And yet, as she turned back into the flat, Will's smiling face and laughing eyes came into her mind, and her heart warmed at the thought of him.

In the flat, June and Eleanor Martin and the twins were talking with Keith's father who was looking more like his old self.

'But what exactly is the 'Blue Riband'?' June was asking.

'This year, it's an actual trophy for the fastest trans-Atlantic crossing,' Mr Watson told them.

Their interest had been sparked off by Harry's remarks about his next newspaper article, and a lively discussion continued.

* * *

By ten o'clock everyone had gone except Mr Wingrave. It puzzled Esther, for he wasn't the type to be last to leave. But he smiled happily when the doorbell jangled.

'That will be my friend Cornelius Conway, the editor of *The Clutha News*. He promised to try to drop by.'

Harry dashed out to open the door, impressed that Mr Wingrave had remembered his promise to contact this man.

A very tall, sandy-haired man in a belted trenchcoat studied Harry.

'So you're the boy wonder Nathan Wingrave keeps pestering me about? You must have some talent when *The Clarion* takes two of your articles. Can you do shorthand and typing?'

Harry looked suspiciously at the big man to see if he was pulling his leg. Then he shook his head.

'Only girls take those subjects,' he mumbled.

'On the contrary, you're no use to me if you can't take down speech accurately in shorthand, reproduce it well and type it out quickly, ready for the press,' the man told him, and Harry was immediately convinced.

'I'll study them at night-school then,' he offered, quickly realising this could be his only opportunity and that he mustn't waste it.

'Just a minute!' Robbie interrupted dourly. 'What are the long-term prospects for him? No-one from this street works for a newspaper.'

'Ah, Mr Johnstone — I believe you're a plater at Burnham's? Just like my father, and my two older brothers.' Cornelius Conway shook Robbie's hand. 'My father wasn't keen on the newspaper trade either, but if the lad works hard he can go far. I've done my bit on the big names, but my wife's an invalid and when I got the chance to edit *The Clutha News* — well, it suits my home circumstances.'

He told them that he had been due to go into the shipyards like his brothers, but a school teacher had got him a start in a big newspaper office.

Finally he rose to his feet and made to leave, but first he turned to Harry again.

112

'Give me enough for a single column on your brother passing his medical exams, and how friends and relations came to congratulate him. Have it ready for next week's edition.'

At the kitchen door he paused to instruct Harry further.

'And be ready, from next week, to go three nights a week to Miss Maggie Lindsay's business college. I'll make the financial arrangements. She's a tartar, but you'll learn shorthand and typing quickly there. If you come up to scratch, you'll get a start after the Fair with *The Clutha News*.'

He winked at Robbie. 'Now we'll see how keen he is when hard work's involved.'

Esther could see from her youngest son's shining eyes that he'd got his heart's desire.

Long after the family had gone to bed Esther and Robbie sat on by the dying fire.

'We've got a son who's a doctor,' Robbie said, shaking his head in disbelief. 'And to think he has a place as an assistant to Dr Angus in Clydebank, starting at two-hundred-and-fifty pounds a year!'

His pleasure and pride in his eldest son soothed Esther's spirits, although Andrew had confided in her that he'd have liked some hospital experience before going into general practice — but he knew it was a luxury that was beyond him.

'Andrew deserves it all,' she murmured.

'Yes. I had my doubts, though, Esther. Folks like us don't usually become doctors,' Robbie conceded.

Esther smiled and nodded. She knew Robbie had been worried that if Andrew failed at university, having rejected starting an apprenticeship, he himself would have been thought a fool who'd got above himself by allowing his son to go to university.

'That Cornelius Conway sounds sensible.' Robbie observed reflectively, having been reassured by Cornelius's ship-building background. 'And he knew exactly what he wanted from young Harry.

'I suppose if the boy does as he's been asked, we'll have to let him take the opening he's been offered. He's nearly fifteen now, so he'll have a year to see if it suits him before the start of an apprenticeship.'

It was the first time he had spoken favourably about Harry's ambition but Esther was careful not to look too excited but rather just to nod her agreement.

'And Eddie Watson told me he'd got a letter for Liz from Keith,' Robbie said, sounding pleased, but Esther kept her thoughts on the Watson family to herself.

She felt that Keith Watson considered Liz an optional extra in his life, and Esther wanted more than that for her only daughter. She was such a decent girl. She deserved better.

Robbie was chuckling now, unusually talkative.

'I overheard Liz and Andrew discussing going to the Malmaison next Friday night. She was telling him to phone up and make a booking.'

'It's her present to him for getting through his finals,' Esther added. 'That new man in costing, Will Robertson, goes there and Liz has heard him talk about it. Funny though — they've been planning to do this since Andrew started university.'

Even going out for high tea was a big treat for Robbie and Esther, and he marvelled at two of his children venturing to the foremost restaurant in town, patronised by royalty and film stars.

★ ★ ★

That next Friday evening, Andrew and Liz sat on the top deck of a red tram going into town. Patiently Liz went over how to act in the Malmaison.

'I'll go to the ladies' powder-room with my coat, and you check in your things at the kiosk and wait for me.'

'Then the head waiter meets us and I

say we've booked a table,' Andrew answered, as if repeating a lesson. 'And if we're offered a drink beforehand I'll opt just to have wine with the meal. Isn't that right?'

'Yes, and with the wine-list you choose the one you want and give the wine-waiter the number,' Liz reminded him.

'Or I can order a half-bottle of the house wine — red if we are having meat, and white if we settle on fish or chicken.'

Liz nodded seriously, and they looked at one another in some anxiety before their sense of the ridiculous overtook them and they broke into peals of laughter. For years they'd jokingly planned to do this when Andrew passed his finals — and now it was a reality.

'How does this Will Robertson in your office know all about the Malmaison?' Andrew asked.

Liz shrugged. 'I don't really know. He never talks much about himself, though he did once mention that his grandparents live in Southbrae Drive.'

Andrew's eyebrows went up at the mention of the elegant stone villas far removed from Yarrowholm Street.

'They're probably the housekeeper and chauffeur-gardener,' Liz commented.

She rummaged in her handbag and gave him four single pound notes.

'That's far too much!' he protested. 'The set meal's ten shillings and sixpence each, then with the wine and a tip the bill shouldn't come to more than three pounds.'

Liz pushed his hand away with the extra note.

'Better hold on to it, just in case,' she said brightly.

Liz was feeling especially happy. This week a couple of warmly affectionate letters had come in the post from Keith. She knew them almost by heart and little phrases kept running through her mind. He thought of her constantly, he'd said, and a new side of him had been revealed by those tenderly written words from the heart.

When the tram reached Central Station Bridge, Liz quickly freed the long skirt of her evening dress which she had hitched up under her coat.

It was the first evening dress she'd made, copied from a picture, and she was a little nervous as to whether it would pass muster in the Malmaison, although Eleanor Martin had warmly approved of it.

'Is this bow-tie still straight?' Andrew whispered as they walked up Hope Street. He was wearing a dinner-suit given him by Dr Dugald, who had outgrown it.

Liz giggled a little as she nodded. Andrew was as nervous of this new experience as she was.

They negotiated the circular revolving doors without mishap, and a figure in a dinner-suit stepped forward to greet them. Liz gasped as Will Robertson smiled down at her, his unruly hair for once neatly brushed.

'I take it this is Andrew? Or should I

say Dr Johnstone?' He shook Andrew's hand warmly. 'We've just arrived too. Come and meet my grandparents.'

Before either of them could respond, he was introducing them to an elderly couple. His grandmother, Mrs Cunningham, wore a loose black beaded gown, and his grandfather was imposing in a dinner-suit, with a gold Albert and chain hanging across his waistcoat.

'So at last we meet, Miss Johnstone. I do hope you will allow me to call you Liz. Will is forever singing your praises,' Mrs Cunningham said, covering Liz's hand in both of hers and smiling happily into her face.

Liz felt sudden colour jump to her face as she tried to answer politely. Somehow she had the feeling that this lovely old lady thought she and her grandson were close, while she knew the only closeness they really shared was when he teased her — though she had to admit that since they'd been working on costing together, she had grown to respect Will's approach to his rather difficult job and had dropped her hostility.

Now her hand was being warmly pumped up and down by Will's grandfather.

'Your brother was one of my better students. It's no surprise that he never had a re-sit, the way he applied himself.'

Liz glanced at Andrew for help, and saw he looked almost as shocked as she felt.

'This is Professor Cunningham who was on the examining panel,' he explained hoarsely.

'I believe you're having a celebration meal? Why not join us as our guests? It'll make a jolly party with five of us.' Professor Cunningham didn't wait for their agreement, calling the waiter over to arrange the change.

As Andrew and Liz went in a daze to leave their coats, Andrew whispered to his startled sister, 'Why didn't you tell me that Will Robertson was sweet on you?'

The Wrong Conclusion?

On Saturday morning, Burnham's narrow ladies' cloakroom was crowded. Laughing, Liz held up a hand for silence and patiently explained what she had been asked to do.

'Will Robertson's grandmother asked me last night if any of my friends . . . you three — ' she indicated the McDonald sisters ' — and of course you, June, and myself would come to the Silver Jubilee Charity Ball in the City Chambers. She'd like us to help with the auction they have at the interval.'

'And it won't cost us anything?' Sylvia asked. She was saving hard for her wedding.

'Not a thing!'

'Are you sure?' Lindsey, the youngest McDonald, queried.

'Will's grandfather is funding a table

for twelve. So besides us there's to be Will Robertson, our Andrew, the twins, and Sylvia's Greg if he wants to come. We're needed to fetch and carry the items to be auctioned then collect the payment. That's the only time we're needed.'

'So we'll be at the banquet, and the dance afterwards, like the other guests?' Fiona, the middle McDonald sister, breathed, her face alight.

'Yes. Mrs Cunningham specially wants young people there to help liven things up.'

June Martin was delighted at the prospect.

'It'll be lovely to see the Glasgow City Chambers. I've heard the marble stairways and banqueting hall are outstanding,' she told the others.

'Greg doesn't have the full dinner tails and white. He's only got a dinner suit,' Sylvia suddenly wailed.

'Mrs Cunningham wants the boys in dinner suits,' Liz assured Sylvia with a twinkle in her eye. 'She says there'll be enough stuffed shirts there.'

'Is Mrs Cunningham one of these formidable committee women?' Lindsey asked.

'Oh, no! She's very gentle and quietly spoken.' Liz smiled, then added, 'Look, we'd best get to our desks, it must be fully nine o'clock!'

As they dispersed, Liz called after the McDonald sisters, 'Sylvia, let me know this afternoon if you and Greg are definite.'

As Liz took her place, Will glanced at her.

'I hope my grandmother hasn't asked too much of you.' He shook his head in amazement. 'I was surprised how quickly she and Andrew put their heads together and got this organised. He had no hesitation about agreeing. How did the rest react?'

Andrew's instant enthusiasm to help at the ball had surprised Liz, too. But this morning her other brothers had been quick to see it as a chance for him to be with June Martin and had teased him accordingly!

'They're all willing,' Liz assured him. 'I'll phone your grandmother this afternoon to finalise the arrangements.'

Liz felt a little uncomfortable with Will now, after detecting last night in the Malmaison that his grandmother thought they were 'special' friends.

'It was very kind of your grandparents to make Andrew and me their guests,' she said stiffly, wanting to refer to it, yet unsure of how to go about it.

'My grandmother's generally several moves ahead of the rest of us. I think the instant she saw you two last night she earmarked you to help,' he commented in a fondly amused tone, then he stood up. 'Come on, let's go and check when the engines for the Two-seven-two are due to go for trials.'

He handed her a brown linen coat and shrugged himself into his own.

* * *

After a month of regular visits to the yard, Liz was becoming familiar with it.

She loved the smell from the braziers where the riveter's boy heated the rivets. And now she recognised the melodic clang of the platers with their right- and left-hand helpers hammering the plates perfectly in turn, one after the other. And she pretended not to hear the ever-impudent red-leaders, who shouted bold remarks to her as they applied special protective coatings to the hull.

A tall workman, his clothes spattered with the red-lead paint, addressed her.

'I see you're visiting the yard regularly now, Liz.'

'Hello, Andy. You're looking well,' she greeted him. 'How's your mother — and the family?'

'The two girls are married, and the boys have apprenticeships,' he told her with quiet pride.

'You've done well by them all,' Liz murmured.

'I'm gaffer of the red-leaders, so I've got steady work now, too.' He gave a wry smile. 'And it helps to be six foot and not afraid of threats, heights or filthy work!'

Liz knew the red-leaders were famed for showing little respect to anyone, especially a boss, so he had an exacting job.

'Who was that?' Will asked as they moved on.

'Andy Knox. He was the cleverest boy in the school. His mother's a widow. Andy was the eldest, so he became a labourer at fourteen to support the family. And he's done it ever since.'

Will nodded with a sympathetic grimace. It was often the case that only the younger members of a family could take the small starting pay of the apprentice, while the eldest had to take the higher wage of any dead-end job to help the family finances.

'Not only clever but a man of good taste, too,' Will commented. 'He's another one carrying a torch for you.'

Liz glanced quickly at him, puzzled by the remark. Was he teasing her again? Everyone knew Andy Knox was simply a boy from her schooldays. Indeed, half the young men in her class now worked for Burnham's in some capacity or other.

She remained silent, deliberately ignoring his remark.

They went into the engine shop, where the marine engineers could be recognised from their peaked ship's engineers' caps. Even some of their apprentices wore them to proclaim their status, too.

Liz stood quietly, ready to take notes, as Will questioned the chief engineer. Then he led the way back through the dust and din from the caulkers' pneumatic hammers, which made even the summer sunshine seem hazy today.

It fascinated Liz how caulkers' teeth always looked so startlingly white in their faces, made black from caulking joints to make watertight seams.

They walked to the open-sided platers' shed to consult her father.

'We've finished with the boilers for

the Two-seven-two and they're being installed,' Robbie told him and gave Will a run-down on the ship's progress.

Then he turned to Liz, his eyes twinkling.

'I see there was another letter arrived from Keith this morning. They're fair steaming in twice a week now.'

'He expects to be home at the beginning of September — ' Liz began, but Will had turned abruptly and walked away, and she had to hurry after him as he made for the slipway where ship 272 was nearing completion.

'Before she was launched, the Queen Mary was called the Five-three-four. Was that because she was the five-hundred-and-thirty-fourth ship to be built in John Brown's?' Liz asked.

'Clever girl! And this is Burnham's two-hundred-and-seventy-second ship on the stocks.'

Will's tone was sarcastic and Liz felt the colour rise to her face.

That was it! She'd had enough. She wasn't going to give him another opportunity to be smart at her expense. Her held high with dignity, she walked purposefully away from him towards the time office.

Will quickly realised the error he'd made. Teasing she could cope with, but sarcasm was going too far. He hurried to catch her up.

'I'm sorry. Forgive me. That was uncalled for.'

'Yes, it was!' Her mind was made up. She would never ask anything of him again. Ever!

* * *

At dinner-time Esther met her daughter at the front door and beckoned her into the big room.

'I'm worried about Harry,' Esther said urgently after she'd closed the door. 'That woman who runs the business classes told him last night that he'll never master shorthand and typing in time. Could you help him? Getting that start with *The Clutha News* after the holidays means so much to him.'

'You want me to give him extra coaching?'

'Would you?' Esther sighed. 'And if only there was a typewriter where he could get in some practice.'

Liz had been so thrilled this morning by the wonderfully romantic letter from Keith that she hadn't noticed young Harry was anxious.

She thought for a minute, then her face brightened.

'I'll take him with me this afternoon to the surgery. Andrew wants me to type some letters for him, and Harry can do the envelopes.'

Esther's face cleared, remembering Andrew's appeal to Liz this morning for help with the surgery's correspondence.

She regretted having to make the request. They all took so much from Liz, and she was unstinting. She never questioned any appeal for help from the family, or from friends for that matter.

'You and Andrew had quite a time last night, getting invited to a ball and being entertained by one of his professors.' Esther was curious. 'Did that Will Robertson not tell you his grandfather knew Andrew?'

'No. He never talks about himself,' Liz answered abruptly, and her mother's eyebrows went up.

'Andrew seemed quite taken with him,' Esther murmured. She was intrigued, and wanted to ask more about this young man, but Liz was unusually reticent, and she realised the matter was closed.

'There's Harry coming now. You can ask him, but don't mention me,' she whispered, and slipped out of the room.

Liz smiled. Her mother always knew who was coming up the stairs, even now when Harry's footsteps were slow and ponderous.

★ ★ ★

Later in the afternoon they swayed in the tram as it clanked its way to Clydebank.

'I never knew shorthand and typing would be so difficult,' Harry complained at Liz's side. 'I'm the worst in the class. All the girls could type by the second lesson — and I can't get the hang of shorthand.'

'You've only had three short lessons,' Liz reminded him. 'And it's easy for girls in offices to get to use typewriters so they get more practise. Don't worry — by the time we've finished, you'll be up to standard.'

'If you say so,' he mumbled, as if he didn't truly believe it.

Dr Dugald's surgery was in a flat behind a chemist shop. Hard wooden benches lined the walls of the gloomy waiting-room.

Andrew was sitting behind the desk in the surgery when they went in.

Liz handed him a pack of sandwiches.

'Mum said you wouldn't have eaten so she's sent these. And while you're eating I'll show Harry how to type the envelopes.'

Liz quickly attended to the letters, then launched into the pile of paperwork, while Harry laboriously addressed envelopes, then did the exercises Liz set him.

By the middle of the afternoon they had made quite a difference and the surgery looked much neater.

'I'd have been at that for hours without you,' Andrew sighed. 'I'm very grateful, Liz. Especially as you gave up a jaunt to town with the girls this afternoon to help me.'

Liz shrugged. 'It isn't a great loss. Lindsey and Fiona are going to get new dresses for the charity ball, which would have been fun — but their mother was coming with us!' she added, pulling a face.

'Olive McDonald will be in her element.' Andrew grinned. 'She won't be able to resist getting Sylvia one, too — and Sylvia won't need to break into her wedding savings.

'By the flow of letters you're getting from Keith, you'll be going the same way soon,' he ventured.

'Better wait till I'm asked,' Liz retorted.

In truth she was amazed by Keith's letters. They were becoming more and more ardent and while she was flattered, she was a little overwhelmed.

She'd given no indication that she felt the same way, and was as confused now about her feelings as he had been when their dates had been such a disappointment.

'Is June looking forward to the ball?' Andrew asked casually.

'Oh, yes. But only because she wants to see inside the City Chambers,' Liz returned, knowing he was keen to discover if he figured at all in June's plans for the evening.

Andrew nodded to Harry whose typing was now measured and rhythmic.

'Sounds as if the lad here is improving,' he said with satisfaction.

Half an hour later they all got off the tram at the foot of Yarrowholm Street, where they met the McDonald family coming home from the town.

'Guess who we met? Will Robertson! And he took us for afternoon tea.'

Fiona McDonald was full of the unexpected meeting, and talked about it all the way up the stairs to their top flats.

Liz wondered if all Fiona's fuss about Will was to make Andrew jealous. She hoped it was for, strangely, the idea of Fiona setting her cap at Will was distasteful.

Once they were in the house and the door was closed, Andrew shook his head.

'I doubt if Fiona's dreams will come to anything. I wouldn't be surprised if he bumped into them on purpose, thinking you'd be there. He hung on your every word when we met in the Malmaison.'

Liz frowned and turned away quickly as if she hadn't heard. She wasn't sure how to react to those hints about Will Robertson's interest.

She thought wryly that Andrew would soon change his opinion if he'd witnessed Will's sarcasm in the yard earlier that day.

But she put such thoughts to one side as she hung up her jacket and joined Harry and her mum in the kitchen.

★   ★   ★

Every free moment in the following days, Liz and Harry worked on his shorthand lessons. Harry was convinced he wouldn't master it in time. But Liz was just as determined to prove he could and gradually he began to improve.

★   ★   ★

On the Friday afternoon, on the day of the charity ball, it was just after dinner-time. Mr Nigel, dapper as ever, was half-sitting on his high stool, his war-wounded leg dangling over the edge.

'It's just a few weeks till Mr Standish, our chief cost clerk, retires. We'll have to give some thought to a gift, and of course a little party, since he's been with the firm for fifty years.' He looked from Liz to Eleanor Martin. 'A gold watch is the usual gift, with a cup of tea and some cakes and sandwiches to follow. Have you ladies any other suggestions?'

All staff presentations took that form, and Liz had never thought of the format being changed.

'I believe he plays bowls. Wouldn't it be a gesture to his enjoying his retirement if he was given a set?' Eleanor Martin suggested. 'And after fifty years' service, surely we could venture a little buffet, with canapés and savouries?

Both Liz and Mr Nigel stared at her, intrigued. Her proposals were outwith Burnham's office staff's usual experience.

'No-one here has ever organised a buffet with canapés,' Liz commented.

Mr Nigel was nodding his head, considering the suggestions, and he enquired how it could be done.

Eleanor explained how simple it would be to organise.

Liz always felt gauche and somehow inept when she listened to the efficient secretary. Eleanor had such an awareness of a wider world which made Liz realise how restricted her view on life was.

'Would you ladies stay here and work out how we could do it? And sound out the opinions of the others, too? I'll take the ideas to Mr Burnham later this afternoon.' Mr Nigel nodded and went out, leaving them in possession of his office.

The gesture amazed Liz. This room had always been so much part of his kingdom. But Eleanor Martin gave no sign of it being unusual.

The two women worked together and as Eleanor knew exactly what was needed it took them less than ten minutes to complete the task.

'You've made it seem so easy,' Liz marvelled. 'Of course, you've had such a varied life.'

'Yes, and most of it unhappy. I knew so few people I could trust,' Eleanor admitted unexpectedly. Then she smiled. 'But strangely, I've found a new contentment here in the office, and in the Yarrowholm Street flat. For the first time in my adult life I feel in control of things . . . ' She stopped, and shook her head in self-mockery.

'Oh, dear, I sound so solemn, especially as I so loathe the boring, daily business of looking after ourselves.' She laughed. 'Thank goodness June has turned out to be a real little housewife. She cleans out the fire as Andrew instructed, and the cooking range has become her pride and joy.'

Liz knew that before June's father died, she and her mother had lived in hotels, or had servants to look after them. But when he had left them only debts, their lives had changed.

Eleanor seemed disposed to chat and

she continued with some amusement.

'We had a visit from Miss Agatha Wingrave from upstairs last evening. She informed us that we have to share the cleaning of the outside entry stairs with those two little ladies next door.'

Eleanor laughed, as if it was of little significance, but Liz was alarmed. Obviously Eleanor didn't realise how important this was in Yarrowholm Street.

'You must go and see the Miss Fosters. They've obviously gone to Miss Agatha and complained,' Liz warned seriously. 'It's a rule of the close to take your turn of the stairs.'

'But I see them washing down Miss Wingrave's flight,' Eleanor pointed out.

Liz hesitated. It was difficult to explain the reasons for this. The Miss Fosters considered themselves genteel, and would never admit to being charwomen, but in fact they did the Wingrave brother and sister's housework several mornings a week.

'They say it's merely an obligement,

because Miss Agatha is in poor health, but the truth is they depend on the money she pays them . . . '

'I see! I'm glad you explained,' Eleanor said gratefully. 'I'll visit them this evening and perhaps I'll . . . ' But she stopped in mid-sentence, and quickly changed the subject.

'By the way, have you heard anything of that lady upstairs who made the secret flight from home?'

'No. We've had no news of Mrs Watson. And Keith hardly mentions her now in his letters.' Liz did wonder about that, for his first letters had been full of his mother. Now he barely referred to her.

'June says you're receiving wonderful letters from him. That's nice for you,' Eleanor observed.

'Yes, it's very flattering — for we only went out the week before he went to sea.' Liz's tone was hesitant.

Eleanor Martin didn't speak for a moment.

'Of course, it's the first time he's

been away from home. No doubt it's all very strange, and he'll be homesick. Everything from his old life will be suddenly very dear to him,' she commented as she gathered up her papers. 'Perhaps when he settles into his new life at sea and starts to enjoy it, you'll find a difference — or then again, maybe not!'

It wasn't what Liz wanted to hear, but her common sense told her it was a wise view that tallied with her own unspoken thoughts.

But she had no time to reflect, for Sylvia McDonald came in just then. Although she was late she gestured excitedly to Liz to go with her to the ladies' cloakroom.

Liz frowned but followed her in.

'Liz! Marvellous news. We've got a room and kitchen in Yarrowholm Street!' Delight shone in Sylvia's face. 'My mother heard about it and went straight to the factor and asked for it. Greg's so pleased because it's near the shop. And it's got a tiled fireplace, and a gas cooker in the scullery . . . '

'Wonderful! And it's exactly where you wanted it. So are your mum and Greg friendly again?' Liz queried.

'Let's say they've called a truce.' Sylvia laughed. 'But Mum is over the moon. She's been so upset recently, wondering why she let herself help Mrs Watson get away.'

Liz nodded her understanding, but Sylvia's thoughts were elsewhere already.

'We think we'll get married in September or October — now that we've got a flat — and I want to be my own boss in my own home.'

Before Sylvia could go on Liz asked her what she thought about the chief clerk's retiral presentation. Sylvia shrugged, too preoccupied with her own plans to bother. Yet when Liz outlined Eleanor Martin's suggestions, she began to grumble.

'She's got Nippy Nigel mesmerised!'

Liz had to agree that after a turbulent start, Mr Nigel and Mrs Martin now worked together most amicably. And it was a fact that he'd mellowed since her arrival.

When she returned to her desk Will Robertson handed her a brown linen coat.

'We need to go down to the yard at once.'

She had planned to do some work with June and wanted to object, and besides, she'd had her hair specially set for the Charity Ball tonight, too, and didn't want dust and grime on. But Will was already holding the door open for her so reluctantly she followed him, feeling annoyed.

On their way to the yard Will stopped and faced her.

'I'm sorry for springing that on you but this is confidential. There's some kind of upset about Eddie Watson. His daughter's here, asking for you.'

Liz stared at him for a moment, questions tumbling over in her mind.

Keith's two sisters took it in turns to clean their father's flat and do his washing. Why should one of them be looking specially for her? Normally, if there was any trouble, it was her mother who would be consulted.

Sudden fear enveloped her heart. Surely it wasn't about Keith?

Will led Liz to a small office where Keith's sister, Jinty, stood waiting, then left them alone together.

'Oh, Liz, you've been getting letters from Keith. Has he said anything about my mother in them?' Jinty asked anxiously.

'Your mother?' Liz swallowed, then shook her head. 'No. Nothing new.'

'I hoped you might know something.' Jinty sat down on a nearby chair, as if suddenly weak. 'A letter came from Keith this morning and I'm sure there was news about my mother in it. But my father won't show it to me. He's just sat hunched at the fire ever since. He won't talk to me.'

Jinty's eyes were moist as she sighed.

'Well — I've got to get back home to Ayr. I'll just have to leave him.'

Liz was at a loss. She didn't know

what was expected of her.

'I'm very sorry,' she stammered. 'Is there anything you want me to do?'

Jinty shrugged and shook her head, also at a loss.

'You know what he's like. He'll not listen to a young person like you. In fact he won't listen to anyone.'

Liz considered this for a moment.

'There is someone he might take into his confidence. He respects Mr Wingrave, the chief loftsman. Perhaps you could speak to him and explain the situation.'

'Would he come here now, privately? The way that young man brought you?' Jinty appealed.

Liz considered the plea and her heart sank. The only person she knew who could go, unsupervised, to the Loft at any time was Will Robertson — and she would have to ask him to take her there.

She would have done anything rather than ask Will Robertson a favour, but this was an emergency.

She went to the time-keepers' office and reluctantly knocked on the door.

Will answered at once.

'What's wrong?' he asked, seeing her troubled expression.

'Jinty's father's had a letter from her mother. Now he's in a kind of numbed shock, and he won't speak to her.' Liz swallowed, and took a deep breath. 'Would you — would you ask Mr Wingrave to come and speak to her . . . ? He's the only one I can think of who might get through to Mr Watson.'

'It could be difficult, this being the last day before the Fair.' Will was frowning and Liz's spirits plummeted. Then he suddenly made up his mind. 'But I think your father could help. Tell your friend we'll be back in a few minutes.'

Very business-like, he started walking towards the yard.

Liz gave a quick explanation to Jinty

148

and hurried after him, all the while hoping her hair, set specially for the ball, wouldn't get too dusty in the yard.

When they reached the platers' shed, her father was giving the crane driver instructions.

'We'll not interrupt. Wait here,' Will instructed, as he made for the office, 'and when he gets a moment, tell him about your boyfriend's father.'

Liz made no sign that she had noticed the 'boyfriend' remark. She'd hated asking Will for help but it was the only way she could assist Jinty.

Five minutes later, Will was back beside Liz, and just as her father came over to join them, Mr Wingrave also appeared.

'Hasn't Keith mentioned anything to you in his letters?' Robbie asked her.

'Not a hint. That's why Jinty's here. She thought I might know something.'

Liz sighed. She didn't point out that, after a period of letters tumbling in at the rate of three a week from Keith, each more passionate than the last, this week she had received none.

'Still, you were only out with him a couple of times before he left. I suppose it wouldn't be proper to give you intimate family news,' Robbie reasoned, and Liz noticed that Will was listening intently to their conversation.

The four returned to the time office, and while Robbie and Mr Wingrave went in to talk to Jinty, Liz and Will waited outside.

'I thought you and this Keith Watson were serious,' Will challenged her. 'That's why I agreed to bring you down here.'

'I've known Keith all my life. The Watsons live downstairs from us,' Liz replied coolly.

'But you're not going steady?' Will insisted.

Liz was by nature completely truthful, and she chose her words carefully.

'Keith asked me specially to write to him.'

Will smiled. 'Well, that puts a different face on things.'

Liz stayed silent, unwilling to enquire what he meant.

Just then, the door opened and the two older men came out with Jinty.

'I'll look in on him on my way home,' Mr Wingrave was saying to a tearful Jinty.

'But I must get home now to Ayr now,' Jinty said anxiously. 'My mother-in-law's looking after the baby for me.'

Robbie Johnstone patted the young woman's arm soothingly.

'Don't you worry! We'll keep an eye on your father, too.'

'Thank you — thank you all very much!' Jinty looked round at them with tear-filled eyes, then she turned and hurried away.

'I'd — I'd appreciate it if you don't mention this in the office,' Liz said earnestly to Will as they walked back together.

'Give me some credit,' Will said dryly.

Friday afternoon was when Liz and June did a trial balance of the week's transactions, and Liz went straight to the high Victorian desk where June was busy.

'I think I've done it!' June gasped, staring down at the page in front of her.

Liz smiled when she'd checked the figures.

'Couldn't have done better myself.'

'I hope Andrew's done as well this week,' June said with a grimace. 'I think he's finding general practice a bit daunting.'

Andrew had obviously confided in June, Liz realised, and she silently hoped that when Keith came home from the sea, they would share that kind of relationship, too.

'I've got the most amazing news,' June whispered, glancing towards Mr Nigel's room. 'I've just heard that Mr Burnham, his wife, Nippy Nigel and my mother will be at the City Chambers tonight, too.'

Liz gulped.

'Will they be at our table?'

June shook her head.

'They're joining another group. Imagine my mother partnering Nippy Nigel!' June giggled. 'That'll set the tongues wagging.'

Liz was dumbstruck. For the couple to be seen so publicly together was like a prelude to an engagement. At least, that's how everyone in Burnham's would view it. And even if Eleanor Martin didn't realise it, Mr Nigel most certainly would.

'Everyone in the yard will know by tomorrow. Don't you mind?' Liz asked.

June's eyes were dancing as she shrugged.

'No, I'm glad. Mummy loves these kinds of occasions. And this last year has been so dull for her. She'll be in her element.'

Liz nodded, and settled down to finish the week's balances.

She'd always thought of Mr Nigel as a dyed-in-the-wool bachelor. Yet he couldn't really be so old. Probably in his early forties, not much older than the elegant Eleanor Martin . . .

A Grand Occasion

That evening, in the kitchen of the Johnstone household, there was near chaos. The twins were trying to tie their bow-ties from diagrams supplied by the dress-hire agency.

Robbie, Greg Scott and Harry all crowded round, attempting to help them, while Sylvia McDonald and Esther looked on, offering encouragement.

Esther's eyes lit up when Liz appeared in the blue evening dress she'd made for the Malmaison night out. She'd brushed out her hair and the softer style suited her.

'You look really bonny,' she murmured.

Then the door bell jangled, and June arrived from downstairs wearing a pale green dress with a white fur cape over her shoulders.

'I'm afraid Andrew hasn't come in yet,' Esther was apologising as the door burst open and he rushed in.

'Give me five minutes,' he called, and disappeared towards the bathroom, giving June a cheery wink on the way past.

Ten minutes later, Esther and Robbie escorted them out of the door, while Olive McDonald came from the opposite flat with her two younger daughters, Fiona and Lindsey, in their finery.

'My! All the girls look like film stars — even Liz!' Olive cried expansively.

Her faint praise wasn't lost on Esther, who bit her tongue. Liz was neat in her dress, not showy like the McDonald girls. She drew her folded arms close to her chest.

Yes! Tonight Liz did look striking. Her dress complemented her red hair, and the long black brocade cloak June had loaned her hung in attractive folds over it. Her skin, too, had an attractive glow in the gaslight.

Esther and Robbie stood on the

landing watching as they clattered downstairs, laughing and chatting all the way.

Olive went with them as far as her corner shop, and when they were all out of sight, Robbie stirred.

'Ay, well, I'd best go and see Eddie Watson now.'

Esther sighed and nodded.

She went back into the house and started straightening the chaos, but she couldn't relax. This latest bother with Eddie Watson was upsetting.

However, Robbie was back quickly.

'Did he say anything to you?' Esther asked.

'No. But he was calmer,' he said, easing into his armchair. 'He said he was having his meal, so I didn't go in.'

Esther sat down opposite him.

'Jinty came up here before she went to Burnham's. She was in an awful state. So I went down and tried to talk to Eddie myself. But he kept moaning about his shame, and how could his wife do this to him.'

Robbie listened, trying to understand.

'It makes no sense. And it was never in Jean Watson's nature to shame anyone.'

'What happened earlier when you and Mr Wingrave went to see him?' Esther enquired.

'Nathan Wingrave went in, since he's Eddie's gaffer.' Robbie explained. 'After a few minutes, I heard Nathan shouting.'

Esther stared at him open-mouthed. Their neighbour, Mr Wingrave, was the mildest of men.

Robbie nodded, agreeing with his wife's amazement.

'I know. But Nathan told Eddie some folks would be happy to have his troubles.'

Esther shook her head.

'I wonder what's gone wrong with that family?' she mused, and continued, 'Liz hasn't heard from Keith at all this week.'

Robbie frowned.

'You'd have thought he'd have dropped a hint to her about what this is about.'

Esther noticed it was the first time Robbie had criticised Keith.

'They're a strange family!' Esther murmured, convinced now that to Keith Liz was nothing more than an extra in his life — to be taken up or left down at his whim. And she believed her daughter deserved better.

* * *

I'm really so grateful, my dear,' old Mrs Cunningham whispered to Liz. 'Losing one of the committee was bad enough, but two of them having to go home is unheard of.'

Liz looked up from laying out the papers and tickets for the auction and smiled.

'It's been fun,' she assured her, and indeed she had enjoyed being in the middle of things.

'Actually, you've been more help than the two of them combined,' Mrs

Cunningham confided with an impish smile. 'But you must stop now and have something to eat,' she insisted as a waiter pushed in a trolley, laden with silver-domed dishes.

'Gran! You're the limit!' Will exclaimed as he burst into the room. 'Liz has missed the banquet and the speeches.'

His grandmother dismissed him airily as she set a plate before Liz.

'She's enjoyed this just as much!' she declared. 'Now don't interrupt. We've only ten minutes to have something to eat before the auction starts. And you should be setting out the goods. Start on these.'

She indicated some paintings and vases on the opposite table.

Liz bent her head and continued eating, enjoying Will's discomfiture as he groaned and did as he was told.

'Save some dances for me,' he whispered as he passed her.

'You'll have to join the queue,' Liz quipped, feeling an unaccustomed confidence.

It was exciting suddenly to find herself being consulted by everyone who came in and out of the committee room. It was as if in evening dress she had become a different person.

When the auction got under way, she was Mrs Cunningham's main helper, and half an hour after it finished, she had everything carefully totalled and checked.

'It's such a boon to have a professional like Liz working with the committee,' Mrs Cunningham said happily to Will, who was back again. 'We'd never have got finished so quickly otherwise.'

'But now I've come to wrest Liz from your clutches, Gran!'

And Will firmly steered Liz out of the room with his hands on her waist.

'I didn't mind,' Liz assured him. 'I enjoyed it.'

'Poor Liz, ever the willing workhorse,' Fiona McDonald said as they came to the table. Then she jumped up to grab Will's arm. 'The slow foxtrot

— my favourite dance. Come on, Will!'
And she pulled him out on to the dance
floor.

Sylvia watched them with a jaun-
diced eye and shook her head.

'Fiona's wasting her time trying to
interest Will,' she remarked as she and
Greg got up to dance.

As Fiona and Will took to the floor,
Liz sat down beside June, who was
watching the party at the other side of
the ballroom where her mother was
seated with Mr Nigel.

'Oh, look, Liz! Nippy Nigel's asked
Mum to dance. She'll enjoy that. She
loves dancing.'

They watched curiously, wondering
how their boss would manage with his
artificial limb. But he exuded a quiet
confidence as he guided the elegant
woman round the floor.

The twins had turned out to be
surprisingly accomplished ballroom
dancers, and Liz was soon enjoying
herself, too, as her brother Frank
swung her round the floor, and Jim

sailed smoothly by with Lindsey McDonald.

Andrew had never had time to perfect the skill, so he and June were making slow progress, but they were so deep in conversation that it didn't seem to matter.

Liz watched a little enviously. Would she and Keith ever be like that — so oblivious of everyone?

Near the end of the evening, there was a roll on the drums and the band leader came forward to make an announcement.

'Ladies and gentlemen. By special request — 'The Grand Old Duke Of York'.'

Will was at Liz's side in an instant.

'Right, this is mine! I haven't been able to get near you all evening!'

Liz laughed, feeling strangely light-hearted. This evening she had discovered a part of herself she had never known before — and she liked what she had found.

As she moved past her on to the

floor, Sylvia whispered in her ear, 'It was Will who requested this.'

Soon the party game was in full swing and the two lines skipped along in high spirits, with loud shrieks piercing the air as couples were caught going through the arch and had to kiss to earn their freedom.

It was only near the end, when Andrew and June were making the arch, that it was brought down on Will and Liz.

His arms tightened around her and his lips found hers, and when they were released, Liz was trembling.

She had never been kissed like that before. It was a disturbing new experience — and she wasn't sure why.

* * *

On Fair Friday, everyone in Burnham's was busy, trying to clear their desks for the annual trades' holiday fortnight.

June and Liz silently totalled up columns of figures, then almost simultaneously drew their double ink lines before gently pressing blotting paper on them.

'Finished!' Liz exclaimed, and straightened up to look at the clock. 'Now we can get on with the buffet for Mr Standish's retiral with a clear conscience.'

While they were unwrapping the plates of food to make an appetising spread, Eleanor Martin came hurrying through from her office to tell them the plans.

'Will Robertson is going to take Mr Standish round the yard to say his goodbyes. He'll keep him there till three. Then we'll have the retiral presentation and buffet until four, when the men will be paid and get off early. All right?'

She returned to her office and closed the door.

'Guess what?' June asked when she heard the typewriter start up again. 'Mummy and I are going down to Kirn next week, as Mr Nigel's guests. He's promised to take us out on his boat.' She put a finger to her lips. 'Don't tell anyone, though.'

Liz was intrigued. So she had been right! There was definitely something going on between those two — which was certainly more than she could say for herself, she reflected sadly.

It was three weeks now since she'd had a letter from Keith, and it was bewildering. She knew there was nothing wrong with the mail service from the ship he was on, for others she knew were getting letters from their sweethearts who were also aboard.

'They're the most unlikely pair!' June giggled as they laid out the savouries. 'But I hope something comes of it. Mummy needs someone she can depend on.'

At three o'clock the foremen and some of the senior tradesmen including Robbie Johnstone came up to the office for the retiral presentation. A photographer from *The Clutha News* was there, too, taking flash photographs, making everyone blink.

Mr Burnham presented Mr Standish

with a fine gold watch, having decided not to break with tradition by giving him the bowls that Eleanor had suggested.

The gentle, white-haired man made a short speech in reply, recalling how things had been done back in 1885 when he'd first started at Burnham's as a boy, and he looked forward to his successor, Will Robertson, making the radical changes that progress demanded.

After the speeches, as Liz handed round plates for the buffet, she was astonished to hear some of the foremen grumbling about Will Robertson's rapid promotion to chief cost clerk.

'Mr Burnham says he doesn't like to break with tradition, but Bobby Douglas served his time here and he shouldn't have been passed over for a newcomer like Will Robertson,' someone growled.

Andy Knox, the head red-leader, was agreeing, but then his face lit up as Liz offered him some savouries and he broke off to speak eagerly to her.

'My mother's taken a house in Millport for the Fair.' He dived into an inside jacket pocket and handed her a piece of paper he had ready. 'Your father says you always have a day in Millport. Here's the address — come and see us, maybe even stay for a bit. My sister's room has an extra bed.'

Although she had known Andy's family all her life, and she and Andy had been at school together, the unexpected offer took Liz's breath away.

She put the paper into her pocket, and tried to smile.

'That's very kind of you. We'll certainly pop in if we're down,' she said rather shakily, and moved on with the plates.

She was in a daze. She couldn't ignore the implications.

Of course, Will had hinted that Andy was attracted to her, but she'd put it down to Will's usual teasing. If only, she thought wistfully, it was Keith making the same offer.

She was still handing round the laden plates when Will entered the room and she happened to catch his eye.

They hadn't spoke since their unexpected embrace at the ball and Liz wasn't sure what to expect, but she steeled herself for the usual teasing. Just the memory of that evening unsettled her.

She was concerned, too, to discover that Will might face opposition in his new post as chief cost clerk. There were many in the yard who believed promotion should always go to a time-served Burnham man.

Bobby Douglas tugged at Liz's sleeve.

'Are the McDonalds going to the Isle of Man again this year?' he asked.

She turned to him in surprise.

'Yes, they're going to Ramsey.'

'Good! So am I!' He grinned. 'Fiona will get a surprise — ' He looked as if he was going to say more, but then he turned quickly back to the buffet, a strange look in his eyes, as Will came over.

It made her uneasy. Did Bobby, too,

resent Will being given the chief cost clerk's job?

Yet it was a foregone conclusion. The costing system needed modernising, and Will had been brought into Burnham's specifically to do it.

'Your young brother's outside the office door,' Will murmured as he passed her.

Liz made her way through the crowd and found Harry on the landing at the top of the stairs.

'Liz! I've passed! And Cornelius Conway has just said I can start with *The Clutha News* after the Fair as a cub reporter.'

Impulsively she hugged him.

'Oh, Harry, that's fantastic!'

'If you hadn't helped me ... I'll never forget it, Liz,' he mumbled, redfaced with emotion, then, totally embarrassed, he fled back down the stairs.

Liz was delighted. She'd made him work so hard at every free moment these last weeks, and it had paid off.

And in truth, all the effort had benefitted her, too, for it had left little time for her to brood over the lack of letters from Keith.

Now she dreaded the Fair holidays and the time she would have on her hands.

She longed for the day when Keith's wonderful letters would start coming again. Why had they stopped so suddenly?

She reasoned that it must have something to do with the news his father had received, yet Eddie Watson was back at work, looking almost normal again.

*　*　*

Soon the men started to stray back down to the yard, and her father gave a huge wink as he passed.

'I got the grand news about Harry! And I've got word of a holiday for all of us!'

'That sounds mysterious!' Fiona

McDonald teased at Liz's side.

Liz shrugged. Everyone knew they never went on holiday. Every penny had had to be saved to support Andrew's medical studies.

However, the holiday mood had taken hold and she couldn't resist teasing her friend.

'You'll have some welcome company in the Isle of Man — ' she told her. 'Bobby Douglas is going to Ramsey, too!'

Fiona's face was a study.

'Oh, no! Not Bobby! I want to meet my Fate there.'

It was nearly five o'clock when Liz was finally ready to leave for the fortnight. All the others had gone and she walked home alone.

When she got into the close, Eleanor Martin was speaking to the two Miss Fosters at their front door.

'I'd be so grateful if you would look after things while we're away . . . '

'We're always happy to do an obligement,' they chorused back, and

Liz smiled to herself. Eleanor had learned the formula for asking very well. The Miss Fosters only did 'obligements' when they were made to feel their assistance was crucial. Money was never mentioned — although, of course, expected!

She walked slowly up the stairs, and was tempted to knock on the Watsons' door to ask if Keith had written to his father in the last three weeks. But she went on and, before she got to the top landing, Harry came running out of their front door.

'Liz! Liz! Guess what? We're going on holiday tomorrow. Cornelius Conway's offered Dad his house outside Anstruther.'

'So you've heard!' Robbie said with a grin as Harry dragged her into the kitchen. 'I thought we deserved a treat and we can manage it this year now that Andrew's graduated.'

'And we're coming for the second week,' Jim announced with some satisfaction. He and Frank would be under canvas at the YMCA camp site at Lochgoilhead with other Burnham's apprentices for the first week of the Fair.

'Everybody says we're going, but there's not a case packed,' Esther interrupted tartly.

She was wary of impulses. Holidays were something she thought should be prepared for and pleasurably anticipated for weeks in advance.

'I'll help you, Mum,' Liz said quietly and without enthusiasm.

She still had a lot on her mind from work. The resentment in the yard about Will's promotion and the dearth of letters from Keith were upsetting. And on top of that, Andy Knox's invitation had been an unwelcome further complication. Still, at least now she had an excuse for not accepting and that was something, she reflected wryly.

'I told Will where we're going, and he says he'll come through and see us. He's going with his grandparents to St Andrews,' Harry told them excitedly.

'That'll be nice!' Esther beamed. 'I'd like to meet him.'

Andrew had told her about Liz's colleague and Esther was a great one for putting two and two together — but Liz refused to meet her smile.

'It's a good thing the washing and ironing are up to date. It's just a matter of putting things into suitcases,' she observed.

It was almost midnight when the cases were finally lined up in the lobby ready for next day.

'You don't seem very enthusiastic,' Robbie remarked quietly to his daughter as she was going to bed in the big room. 'Don't worry, I've arranged an obligement with the Miss Fosters to send on any mail.'

'Something serious must have happened,' Liz murmured.

'Maybe Keith's had as big a shock about his mother's news as his father did,' he observed, and Liz looked at him sharply.

'You know what happened?'

174

He nodded. 'Eddie Watson finally opened up tonight. I haven't told your mother yet. She had enough on her mind getting ready for the holiday.' He paused then took a deep breath. 'You'd best prepare yourself for a surprise . . .'

★ ★ ★

'A baby! His own flesh and blood and he's acting as if it's all Jean's fault!' Esther Johnstone was incensed at the attitude of the man. Robbie had just given her the news of Jean Watson's pregnancy.

Robbie held up a placating hand.

'It's something Eddie Watson will have to work out for himself.'

'But that poor woman, going to Canada on her own and a baby on the way . . .' Esther paused, suddenly recalling the conversation she'd over-heard. 'Of course! That's why she and Olive McDonald talked about Prince's Pier, Tail o' the Bank, Duchess of York and Yorkhill Quay . . .'

Robbie nodded. 'Aye, the places and ships you'd need to know about if you were heading for Canada.'

'But who'd have believed Olive could have kept it secret?'

Esther was amazed for her next-door neighbour usually thrived on gossip.

'Oh, I think Olive took fright when she saw the upset Jean's disappearance caused,' Robbie responded, as perceptive as ever.

'Why didn't you tell me this last night at home?' Esther accused him, as she gestured round the bedroom of their holiday home.

'I wanted this holiday for all of us. If I'd told you last night, you'd have ranted on about it — and maybe been too upset to pack the store-cupboard case,' Robbie murmured, a little smile playing round his eyes. Despite his protests about the extra weight, she'd insisted on bringing a case with food from her store cupboard.

But Esther was too annoyed, fussing about her holiday home and unpacking

176

their suitcases, to realise he was teasing her.

She was quivering with indignation as she put clothes on hangers.

'It's little wonder Nathan Wingrave was so angry with Eddie Watson's attitude. He's a dyed-in-the-wool bachelor and his sister Agatha's not going to marry this side of fifty, and they're the last in the line. When you think what a child would have meant to them . . . '

However, after a moment of reflection, the holiday mood finally got through to her, as Robbie had know it would eventually.

'Och, why should I let Eddie Watson upset our first holiday in years? Look, Robbie, even the sun is shining.'

The Fair Fortnight

Esther was truly delighted with the neat terrace house they'd rented. She knew it was little more than a change of sink for her, but it was all so novel that it would be like playing at housekeeping here.

Going through to Harry's room, she instructed him on what space to leave for the twins coming next week.

Liz was in the tiny box-room, lit by a fanlight window. It only had space for a small bed and a set of drawers but it was cosy and Liz was charmed with it.

'Let's go and explore, Liz,' Harry suggested once he'd completed the tasks Esther had set him.

'Yes. Away you go for a walk. You're looking a bit pale after the train journey,' Esther suggested when she looked up from stacking the storecupboard shelves. She sensed that Keith's unpredictable behaviour was depressing her daughter — even though he was thousands of miles away.

It took Liz a moment or two to summon up the interest to go with Harry. The three-week gap in letters from Keith had lowered her spirits and Andy Knox's unexpected invitation to his mother's holiday house in Millport had confused her. Surely he hadn't taken her interest in his family as encouragement for a romantic interest?

'Let's go down to the beach and hunt for crabs,' Harry suggested excitedly, and Liz and her mother exchanged smiles. Budding journalist he might be, but underneath he was still an excited 15-year-old on his first holiday since he was a child.

'Did you make a wish when we came over the Forth Bridge?' Harry asked as they made their way through the garden that opened on to the beach.

Liz smiled, thinking of the moment when the train had thundered through the steel cantilevers over the waters of the Forth. Everyone had thrown a penny out of the carriage window for luck and she'd wished very specially that Keith would write to her again. How she looked forward to reading those beautifully phrased sentiments . . .

'I wished to meet my Fate, riding on a white charger,' she told him with a laugh as her feet touched the sand.

'I wished, too, but just that we'll have a wonderful holiday!' Harry confessed shyly, then raced on ahead.

The tide was out and brother and sister were soon scrambling over rocks, exploring pools and calling to each other when they sighted anything unusual.

'Come and see this monster!' another voice called — a familiar voice.

Liz looked up, amazed to see Will Robertson, bare-legged, in khaki shorts and open-necked shirt, the breeze lifting his wiry, wavy hair.

'We arrived in St Andrews this morning, and it's only ten miles from here,' Will explained. 'Your father told me where to find you.'

Liz was surprised at how pleased she was to see him. The sight of him had instantly raised her spirits. Away from the office, he was good company, as she'd discovered at the ball his grandmother had organised.

'What kind of car have you got?' Harry asked immediately.

'It's my grandfather's Rover. Come and see it. We could take a run into Anstruther.'

'Oh, I can't — not looking like this!' Liz wailed, glancing down at her damp shoes, seaweed-smeared legs, and smoothing her hair which was blowing about in the breeze.

'You look great to me.' Will grinned, and her colour rose at his frank appraisal.

But then Harry grabbed her hand and pulled her along, and the moment was gone.

'Oh, come on! Don't start the girlish clothes thing. I've never been in a motor-car before.'

'I've only ever been in taxis myself — never a private car,' she answered cheerfully, keen to try this new experience.

* ★ ★ *

In Anstruther they walked round the busy harbour, studying the fishing boats and licking the ice-cream cones Will bought for them all from a man with a brightly-painted ice-cream cycle.

Harry wandered off ahead and Liz found herself alone with Will.

They leaned on the harbour wall in companionable silence, gazing out over the water to where steam drifters bobbed in the sparkling water, making a pleasing picture.

Finally Will broke the silence.

'I met your mother when I arrived at the cottage. She told me about Eddie Watson's attitude to his wife's news. She's quite indignant on Jean Watson's behalf.'

His candour surprised Liz and it

occurred to her that her mother must have had quite a chat with him to reveal her true feelings like that.

'It was a surprise to us all. Yet it explains a lot,' Liz said carefully. 'Mrs Watson loves children, but she probably knew how her husband would react to news of this late baby.'

'Your mother believes she went away to enjoy the baby. But Canada strikes me as an extreme choice,' Will commented thoughtfully. 'How did your Keith discover she was there?' he continued, making an entirely incorrect assumption that he was 'her' Keith.

'I don't know.' Liz shrugged, reluctant to discuss Keith's family problems or to reveal to Will that she hadn't heard from Keith for weeks. 'Mr Watson only said that Keith had written with the news,' she told him and was relieved when Harry rejoined them and the sudden tension was broken.

'There's a fruiterer over there. Mum needs some things. I won't be a minute,' and she hurried off, glad to be alone for a little.

She bought enough fruit and vegetables to last a few days, and took the opportunity to reflect on her tangled feelings.

She was bitterly disappointed by the lack of letters from Keith. She'd idolised him since their schooldays and yearned for the endearing letters and the reassurance that she was still special to him — even more special than she'd ever believed.

And yet, since Will's unexpected arrival here today, she wanted to be carefree, too. She wanted to put her tortured thoughts aside and subdue the nagging belief that if Keith cared he'd have written with an explanation by now.

Later, when Will drove back to the holiday house, Esther was waiting. She'd found a large, heavy girdle in the cupboard and baked a batch of scones.

'I was just about to make a cup of tea. You'll have one before you go back to St Andrews?' she invited him cheerfully.

He immediately pulled out a chair at the kitchen table and sat down.

Liz put away the shopping, knowing her mother enjoyed company and any excuse to have a natter round the table.

The pile of scones on the plate quickly diminished as Harry, Will and her father made short work of them.

Will sat back, replete.

'Delicious, Mrs Johnstone. I won't get fed till dinner in our hotel, which is after seven tonight.'

'Well, now you know the way, you'll be very welcome any time,' Robbie put in.

'I think you'll see me regularly if you have a spread like this on offer,' Will commented with a smile for Esther, and for most days afterwards, he returned and spent an hour or two with them.

The weather stayed pleasant and they found living in the fishing community an enjoyable experience. Their days formed a routine. Most mornings Robbie strolled down to the little harbour and talked with the old seamen while Esther got to know the wives who sat in the sun at the doors of their houses, knitting or darning the fishermen's heavy socks.

At the weekend, the twins arrived from their camping week.

'It was fantastic. We had sports every day. Of course, Frank and I won a three-legged race, and a wheelbarrow race,' Jim crowed. 'We got a big jar of sweets each.'

'And it was our apprentices from the Garscube Harriers who put Burnham's on the map. We were placed in all the races!'

They eagerly showed photographs of the events, and Jim produced the two glass jars, filled with boiled sweets, for their admiration. Then he handed Liz a letter from Keith.

'The Miss Fosters said it came yesterday morning,' Jim said before they continued regaling everyone with stories from their trip while Liz slipped off to her tiny room to enjoy Keith's letter alone.

She sat on the bed and her hands trembled eagerly as she opened it. It was a short letter and to the point as Keith explained how a Canadian cousin had visited his ship with news of his mother. Painfully absent were the loving sentiments that had warmed her heart in his recent letters. This was like the ones she had received at first and she was disappointed.

What had happened to the beautiful phrases of affection she'd craved when she'd thrown her penny from the train on the Forth Bridge? The loving lines had been something tangible from her one week of faltering romance before Keith had sailed off to Canada.

★ ★ ★

The weather broke in the middle of the second week. The family sat in the cosy parlour as rain battered against the window.

Liz took the opportunity to work on the dress she was making to wear at

Sylvia's wedding in September. Harry prowled around, unable to settle. For once even books couldn't hold his attention. Now he stood at the window watching the rain.

'Here's Will's car. He's got his grandmother — oh . . . just a minute — ' He paused as he wiped condensation from his breath on the window. 'I think there's something wrong with the old lady.'

As the knocker was banged frantically Esther was already on her way to the door.

'We were out for a run. My grandmother's taken a turn,' Will blurted out as soon as the door was opened.

'Bring her inside. We'll put her on the couch in the parlour.' Esther was immediately in charge. 'Harry! Go and get the quilt off Liz's bed.'

Will and Robbie gently carried the frail-looking old lady into the parlour. Despite her eyes being closed and her breath coming quickly, she scolded them in a strong voice.

'Don't fuss. I'll be all right in a moment now that I'm out of the car.'

'Quite right!' Esther agreed. 'So all you young ones, out — and that includes you, Will.' She turned and swept them all to the door. 'Liz — put the kettle on!'

In the kitchen Will explained how, since it was raining, his grandmother had asked him to run her to Anstruther, and while they were there she had suddenly complained of feeling strange.

'I didn't know what to do,' he said anxiously. 'My grandfather's in Edinburgh for the day, but since you were so near, I suggested we come here, and she agreed.'

Robbie came back into the kitchen and nodded reassuringly.

'I think it's just car-sickness. An hour's peace and quiet with a cup of tea and she'll be fine. And we've to break out the scones!' he grinned.

Harry let out a cry of joy.

'Will, you've done us a good turn. Usually we're not allowed to touch them till tea-time.'

Liz set a tray with the daintiest china she could find in the cupboard, and put out a selection of scones and some of her mother's special rhubarb jam, then carried it through to the parlour.

'I'm a fraud!' Mrs Cunningham announced as Liz put down the tray. 'There's nothing wrong with me that a cup of tea won't cure.'

'Just leave the tray here, I'll pour,' Esther announced comfortably, and Liz knew she was dismissed.

She smiled to the anxious-faced Will when she went back to the kitchen.

'Don't worry. By the looks of things my mother and your grandmother are settling down for a good old gossip over that pot of tea.'

Will sat back comfortably in the kitchen chair, and gave a sigh of relief.

'What a fright she gave me. But I knew that your mum would cope — that's why I drove straight here.'

Harry brought out the compendium of games.

'Let's have a Ludo championship.'

Now the old lady was being looked after they were all in happy mood.

Will gestured to the seat beside him

'Liz, why don't you come and sit with me to give me luck?'

The holiday spirit took hold of her and she cheered him on when his first roll of the dice was a starting six. She found this carefree side of Will much more attractive than his constant teasing in the office, and she realised that she, too, often directed barbed comments towards him in their war of words. Now it was pleasant to relax and laugh in each other's company.

She was reminded of other rainy afternoons, those in Yarrowholm Street, when Keith Watson had played board games with them. However, he'd never specially requested her to sit next to him then, and if she ever had, she had arranged it herself.

In time the door opened and old Mrs Cunningham and Esther came into the kitchen.

'I feel like a new woman,' the white-haired lady assured them all. 'And now I must return your hospitality. You'll all come for lunch on Friday. I insist on it.' She held up a warning finger. 'The young men can play golf in the afternoon. The hotel has spare clubs and will kit them out.'

'Great idea, Gran,' Will agreed, turning to the family. 'I'll come and collect you. Maybe I'll get my revenge on the Links for the trouncing I've just had at Ludo.'

As they waved the car off, the rain was unabated and Robbie looked up warily at the unpromising sky.

'Hope the weather improves,' he murmured.

'Lunch in a hotel, then golf. What do we wear?' Young Harry was awed. He'd never been inside a hotel.

'Sports jacket and flannels for you men, and summer dresses for me and Liz,' Esther decreed, at her decisive best. 'Neat but not too showy.'

The boys were delighted, yet anxious,

too, about the golf. None of them had played before.

★ ★ ★

Next morning when Will arrived they were all waiting.

'Gosh! You all look so distinguished. Wait till my grandmother sees you! She'll send me back to change and brush my hair!' He grinned, running his hand through his tousled, wavy hair.

The day was sunny with a brisk breeze, and after lunch, Liz accompanied the boys round the course as they played. The twins were natural sportsmen, and soon mastered the instructions Will gave them. Harry was more erratic, but by the end of the round they were all confirmed fans of the game.

In the early evening, Will drove them, sun-burnished and golden, back to the holiday house. It had been a very successful day. Esther had delighted in the novelty of lunching in the hotel, and Robbie had found common ground with Professor Cunningham discussing Clyde-built ships; the professor's father had been a shipyard worker and he retained an interest.

When Robbie unlocked the door, he bent to pick up a piece of paper from the doormat and once he'd read it he passed it to Liz.

'Seems you've had a visitor. Andy Knox was here looking for you.'

All the joy of the day drained away from Liz as she read the note. It was short, just saying that he'd changed his holiday plans and how sorry he was to have missed her but he would see her back at work on Monday.

'And there's another letter from Keith.' Robbie picked up a letter. 'The Miss Fosters have sent it on.'

'All these young men in your life, Liz. How are you going to choose?' Harry chuckled as if it was something of a joke.

'That's enough from you, young man,' Esther said sternly.

One look at Liz's face told her Andy

194

Knox's note was an unwelcome intrusion, and she was annoyed, for it had cast a shadow on a perfect day.

Will, having heard all this, politely declined Esther's offer of tea, making an excuse that he must get back. Esther was doubly disappointed for he'd always willingly stayed before. Now, the only thing that lay before her that evening was packing the family's suitcases.

A little later she went into her daughter's room, and found Liz sitting on the bed, Andy Knox's note on one side and Keith's open letter on the other.

Esther came right out with what was on her mind.

'I didn't know you were soft on Andy Knox.'

'I'm not!' Liz was adamant, and explained about his inviting her down to Millport.

'Do you like him?'

Liz shook her head helplessly.

'I've never given him any thought.

He's just one of the boys from school who works in the yard. When I saw him in the yard I congratulated him on being made a charge-hand. But I was only being polite.'

Esther sniffed and frowned down at the other letter on the bed.

'And what's Keith saying about his mother this time?'

'The baby's due at the beginning of September. His mum's keeping well, housekeeping for her widowed brother and his family. Keith plans to be home in time to be Greg's best man at the wedding.'

As she relayed the facts, her voice was flat, only just hiding her disappointment that it was that kind of letter again.

Esther longed to put her arms around her and have a heart-to-heart talk. She wanted to know about her daughter's feelings about Keith. But she knew she mustn't interfere. Instead she gave a polite smile as she sat down beside Liz.

'I hope Jean Watson gets a bit of happiness out of life,' she began, but something in Liz's expression made her change tack.

'Are you still worried about Andy Knox?'

'I am, a bit,' Liz admitted. Then, after a pause, she confided, 'I heard him with a few others at Mr Standish's retiral party, murmuring that Bobby Douglas should have got the promotion to chief cost clerk instead of Will . . .'

' . . . because Bobby's time-served in Burnham's, and Will isn't? It's an exclusive brotherhood to them.' Esther snorted derisively. 'I don't know why they're bothered. Bobby Douglas will get the job in a year or two after Will's made the changes that are needed. Will's destined for higher things,' Esther said, her tone emphatic.

Liz looked up, interested. She had the feeling that old Mrs Cunningham had confided a great deal to her mother. But Esther, as if realising she had said more than she should,

197

forestalled any questions and stood up.

'It was lovely having the last day out, but it's left a lot to do tonight. I'll get the supper on the go then we'll get packed up for the morning.'

Back To Reality

Glasgow tram drivers were very accommodating about returning holidaymakers, allowing them to pile their cases in their open cabs. Even the odd piece of furniture was carried when necessary.

But Robbie decided that they'd finish their holiday in style and ride home from the station in a taxi. He'd silently hoped it would cheer Liz up as she'd been very quiet since that note had arrived from Andy Knox. She'd been so carefree up till then.

'It's lovely to have you all back. It's been quite lonely over the Fair with everyone away.' The two Miss Fosters, Maisie and Jeannie, were waiting at the top of the steps to the close. 'The McDonalds have beaten you. They were home by Thursday,' Maisie Foster informed them, and her sister bobbed her head in eager agreement, which alerted Esther.

'They weren't due back till tonight. Was it illness?' Esther asked.

'No, no! A matter of the heart, we hear,' Jeannie informed them with a suitably serious face.

'Very upsetting for them!' Maisie nodded solemnly.

Esther and Robbie exchanged glances. Both knew that the Miss Fosters were excited and couldn't wait to pass on the news which added some spice to their lives.

'And Mrs Martin and her daughter have been home since the beginning of the week. They were sailing down at Kirn, we believe,' Maisie said.

'And young Dr Andrew has enjoyed having them back. He had his evening meal with them every night,' Jeannie added. Nothing had escaped the Miss Fosters, Esther observed.

She also realised there must be reasons for being given so much news of the close so quickly and asked them a further question.

'And how about the Wingraves? And Mr Watson?'

There was a small pause, and the two sisters seemed to draw closer.

'Miss Agatha and her brother won't arrive from Nairn till mid-evening. And of course, Mr Watson has stayed at home.' They exchanged a glance. 'We think he's looking for someone to clean and wash for him,' Maisie ended primly.

'But we told him we didn't know of anyone.' Jeannie sniffed.

Esther realised he'd made the mistake of asking them to do it, instead of choosing his words carefully, so that they could look on it as 'an obligement'.

Robbie and the boys came forward with the suitcases, and as they started up the stairs, the Martins' door was flung open and Eleanor, June and Andrew came rushing out to welcome them back.

Esther cut short the conversation.

After two weeks away she was desperate now to get upstairs to her own flat.

'Come up after tea and we'll catch up on all the news then,' she suggested.

An hour later she'd emptied the suitcases and had the washing for Monday put aside, and she was just about to put the cases away when the doorbell interrupted her.

When she opened the door, a woeful Olive McDonald confronted her.

'Esther, would you come over when you've got a minute? I need your advice.'

'I've heard about Jean Watson being in Canada and the baby on the way, if that's what you mean,' Esther reassured her gently, but Olive shook her head and sighed.

'That's common knowledge now. No — it's not the Watsons who are my worry. Please come when you can and I'll tell you all about it.'

'Of course!' Esther nodded, and Olive turned dejectedly and went back over the landing to her flat.

'What do you think about that?' Esther asked Liz, who'd heard every word.

'Haven't a clue. But it must be important to have brought them home from the Isle of Man early.'

Esther sighed. 'I've had such a lovely holiday, and I really don't want Olive spoiling it all with tears. I was looking forward to the Martins coming up. They're always such good company — it would have finished the Fair off nicely.'

When the doorbell rang again Esther looked at Liz.

'You answer it!'

Liz opened the door, and this time it was Sylvia McDonald with tear-filled eyes.

'Can I come in and speak to you privately?'

As soon as they were in Liz's room with the door closed, Sylvia said dramatically, 'It's all over! I've finished with Greg! I refuse to live the rest of my life being ordered around by him

— and I've found out I like Bobby Douglas better!'

Liz stared open-mouthed, hardly able to take it in.

'You mean — you've broken your engagement to Greg?' She gulped. It was an unheard-of event in Yarrowholm Street.

Sylvia nodded, dashing a tear from her eye with the edge of her hankie.

'My mum's furious with me. But I've made up my mind, and Bobby has asked me to be his girlfriend.'

'But — but Keith's coming home in time to be Greg's best man,' Liz said weakly, wondering when she'd ever see him again now.

'I don't care!' Sylvia was petulant. 'I love Bobby — he's so polite and considerate.' Then she stopped and looked at Liz, hysteria not far away. 'You'll help me, Liz — to return the engagement presents — and write to the guests saying the wedding's off, and cancel the church, and caterers, and everything . . . Please say you will . . . '

'What's made her do it? She only got engaged to Greg a few months ago.' June Martin shook her head, bewildered.

Liz shrugged, lifting a plate from the sink on to the drying board, and June rushed on not waiting for a reply.

'I remember Sylvia was on top of the world — she couldn't wait to give up work to be a housewife. And now, to drop Greg and take up with Bobby Douglas, of all people — he's so colourless!'

'Bobby's quiet, but he's very conscientious,' Liz commented, defending Sylvia's new love. 'She says she doesn't want to spend the rest of her life being ordered about by Greg.'

'W . . . what?' June gasped, and she clamped a hand over her mouth to suppress a bubble of laughter.

Liz stared at her, then she, too, saw the absurdity of anyone bossing Sylvia about and had to bite her lip to stop her own giggles being heard out in the kitchen.

June wiped her eyes, gulping an apology.

'Oh, I'm sorry. That was unkind of me, laughing like that . . . '

'No, I'm glad you did,' Liz protested. 'Sylvia's news put a real damper on our homecoming and it's been a tonic having you seeing the funny side.'

Liz had told June of the comings and goings since their return from holiday earlier that evening. How Sylvia had been certain of what she'd decided and asked Liz to organise returning the presents.

'I suppose she won't be handing in her notice at Burnham's now. And that'll cause another upset.' June was suddenly serious. 'I heard Nippy Nigel talking with my mother about a new tracers' department being planned after Sylvia leaves. Her sister Fiona's not to be promoted either. Someone's being brought in from outside. All their long cloakroom discussions on the wedding have told against her.'

Liz stared down at the soapy suds in the sink. This would be an upset for Fiona, who had been taking her promotion for granted.

Fiona's pride had already been dented by Andrew's growing preference for June. She had hoped that when his studies were over he'd have more time for her — but any free time he had was being spent with June.

'I don't know what Keith will think either,' Liz mused. 'The wedding was planned for when he's due home, so that he could be best man.'

Sylvia's actions were having far-reaching effects, and although she laughed with June about it, Liz was quietly appalled at her friend's sudden switching of her affections.

'It seems strange that after such a long time she should find they've nothing in common,' June said. 'Perhaps she realised she was 'in love with love', as my mother said she was when she married my father.'

'Maybe so,' Liz murmured, a little shocked by June's comment. She would never dream of making observations about her own parents' relationship.

But they were always as one, devoted to each other, and until recently she'd thought that all married couples were like that. But what had happened with Keith's parents had shown there were exceptions.

She pushed the uncomfortable thoughts away and changed the subject.

'How did you enjoy your week sailing with Nippy Nigel?' she asked.

'It was lovely,' June replied. 'Mummy and I soon found our sea legs again and we even remembered the correct knots to tie. We once had a sailing yacht in Cannes, but my father had to move on, and that was the end of that!'

She spoke lightly, almost masking the bitterness of the memory.

Liz often felt gauche and plain beside June, although she was six years older. June had experience of a world she barely knew existed.

'It was an education for me, getting to know Nippy Nigel away from the office.' June chuckled. 'He's really rather sweet. His bad leg didn't seem to hinder him at all as he clambered all over the boat. And he was really quite fatherly to me as well.'

'I've always respected him because he's fair,' Liz admitted, although she knew some in the office thought he made petty rules just for the sake of it.

'By the way, how was your holiday?' June queried. 'You haven't said much about it but I believe Will Robertson was with you ... Almost daily from what I've heard.'

June smiled with her head to one side, watching Liz's response carefully.

Liz laughed. 'Now don't you start!'

Being teased about Will Robertson's intentions was becoming a habit. They were just good friends. Anyway, she was counting the weeks till Keith was home at the end of his first voyage.

'Driving out to see us was simply his excuse to borrow his grandfather's lovely motor-car,' Liz explained.

June smiled dreamily.

'It was lovely coming home this week and having Andrew's company in the evening,' she said. 'We talked about everything under the sun. I think I missed him while we were away. Have you had news from Keith?' she added.

'Yes. Two letters came while I was on holiday,' Liz said quickly, but she didn't admit they had been a disappointment, with none of the beautiful sentiments of affection in his earlier correspondence.

'I only saw his mother once or twice when we first arrived in the close. I thought she looked too old to have another baby — yet at forty-three it's not unknown,' June mused, then her eyes danced with mischief. 'Just think, Liz! I could have a little brother or sister if my mother and Nippy Nigel tie the knot. Mum's just thirty-nine.'

'Do you think they will?'

June shrugged. 'I don't know if she could cope with being a housewife.'

They were interrupted as the door

swung open and Andrew came in.

'Come on, you two,' he said breezily, 'you must have washed the supper dishes by now.'

'Just finished!' Liz dried her hands, envying the way June and her brother looked at each other. They'd had eyes for no-one else ever since they'd first met, just months ago.

They all went back into the kitchen just as Eleanor Martin got up to leave.

'It is lovely to have you back,' said Eleanor. 'We did so miss you.'

June laughed. 'When we returned from Kirn there were only the Miss Fosters and that strange Mr Watson left in the close.'

'He was suddenly quite friendly to us,' Eleanor replied, 'after ignoring our existence since we arrived. He told me he wanted his wife to come home after the baby's born.'

★   ★   ★

After Esther and Robbie saw their neighbours out, accompanied by Andrew who went down for a book, Esther popped her head round the bedroom door to check on her youngest son. Harry had gone to his room soon after supper, and she found him sitting up in bed, practising his shorthand skills. It was tomorrow he was starting as a cub reporter with *The Clutha News*.

Esther would be eternally grateful to Mr Wingrave for talking Robbie into letting the boy try.

'I should be able to cope, Mum.' He grinned. 'I'm all ready to cover anything from court cases to tennis dances or the Woman's Guild social.'

Before she could open her mouth to reply, he mimicked her. ''Be ready to sweep the floor and make the tea, my lad!''

While Esther was still laughing Harry asked suddenly, 'Do you think Liz will still end up with Keith? She'd be better with Will Robertson,' he added. 'But she doesn't seem to notice that he's keen on her.'

Esther came further into the room and closed the door, silently recalling that Will's grandmother had been of the same opinion.

'It's something Liz will have to decide,' she said, pursing her lips and stooping to pick up a pile of dirty washing.

Harry chuckled suddenly.

'It looks as if Andrew and June Martin will make a pair. I didn't expect him to fall into the trap — he was always wrapped up in his medical books before.'

'Just you wait, my lad! It'll happen to you.'

'Never! No girl's going to catch me!' Harry scoffed.

'I'll remind you of those words one day,' his mother said with a smile as she left his room and crossed the hall to Liz's.

However, her smile died when she saw Liz's face.

'Oh, Mum! I'm back at work tomorrow, and what am I to do about Andy Knox?' Liz wailed. 'He's bound to make some reference about turning up at our holiday house and us not being there. He must have either changed his holiday plans or made a special journey over to see us — well, me, I suppose,' she corrected.

She looked at her mother helplessly.

'I've given him no encouragement — but how can I let him know I'm just not interested in him?'

Esther dropped the dirty laundry on top of the pile Liz was making from her holiday suitcase and sat down.

'I'm afraid it looks like Andy's determined to court you,' she sympathised. 'You'll just have to be firm.'

They looked at one another in resignation, and Liz nodded glumly.

'I've a feeling it won't be easy.'

'You could imply that you and Keith have an understanding,' Esther suggested but Liz frowned.

'No. He knows Keith only asked me

214

to write to him.'

'So is Andy trying to stake a claim before Keith gets home?' Esther asked, with a hint of humour.

Liz gave a wan smile.

'That's one explanation.' Then, feeling on safer ground, she asked, 'What did Sylvia's mum say when you went over to see her?'

Esther smiled grimly.

'Olive's black affronted. Greg Scott's got his father's butcher's business behind him and was a good solid prospect — while Bobby Douglas is just a clerk at Burnham's. He's the one that your friend Andy believes should have got Will Robertson's job.

'Sylvia refused, point blank, to make it up with Greg. Now, to top it all, Greg is saying to everyone, 'Good riddance to bad rubbish'.'

'Oh dear.' Liz grimaced. 'That makes it nasty!'

Esther leaned forward and patted her daughter's hand.

'It's Sylvia's decision. She took it

without consulting you, me, or her mother, so let her work it out in her own way — and don't you be shouldering her burden. You've enough to think about.'

★　★　★

After the two weeks of tranquillity, the Clyde became a living river again as it growled into life on the Monday after the Fair.

Once again there was the background roar of horns, clanging hammers, and the clatter of riveters' guns from the shipyards that lined its banks from Govan to Greenock.

Liz was scarcely aware of the noise as she walked to work that Monday morning, feeling unusually nervous. Sylvia's broken engagement would complicate life at the office, added to which was her dread that Andy Knox would waylay her at the first opportunity.

She was out of her depth, never

having experienced the unwanted attentions of a persistent suitor.

She was first to arrive, but when she reached her desk, the door burst open and Will Robertson marched in.

'I was in the yard. Is it true about Greg and Sylvia?' he demanded.

Liz nodded, briefly outlining the events.

When she finished, Will gave a low whistle.

'The yard's buzzing with it. And the other great talking point is speculation about Mr Nigel having Mrs Martin and June for a sailing weekend. The talk is that the banns are imminent.' He grinned, running his hand through his wavy hair.

Then Will noticed Liz was still tense and unsmiling.

'Is something bothering you?'

Liz's first impulse was to deny it, but then she caught sight of the concern in his eyes.

'I'm not looking forward to bumping into Andy Knox. He's got completely

217

the wrong end of the stick — and he's very persistent.'

She wondered if Will might offer a suggestion — but his face became distant.

'Oh yes! Especially when you're hoping the elusive Keith will be coming home with an engagement ring!'

There was no hiding the sarcastic tone in his voice and Liz glared at him. Obviously her happy holiday companion had been left in Fife!

Indignantly she hitched herself on to the high stool at the bookkeepers' desk with her back to him.

The swing door went busily back and forth as the rest of the office staff started to arrive. It seemed most of them had heard Sylvia McDonald's news and those who hadn't were regaled as they entered.

A heavy silence greeted the arrival of Bobby and Sylvia and Liz couldn't help overhearing Sylvia remark to him, as he took his seat, 'Remember, Bobby, that job should have been yours. Don't let Will Robertson put the work on to you.

There's a few down in the yard waiting to trip him up as well.'

Liz shook her head. Although Will was for ever baiting her, she respected his competence, and she regretted the antagonism that he would have to face on the first day in his new job.

June slipped on to the stool beside her, and, as she took a ledger down from the brass rail above the desk, whispered carefully to Liz, 'I think we're in for a morning of fireworks! Nippy Nigel knows about the broken engagement and Sylvia's plan not to hand in her notice now. He's going to call her in for a chat — and Fiona, too.'

Liz knew what that meant and glanced quickly at June, but her face betrayed nothing as she busily began entering invoices.

Almost immediately Sylvia was called in to Mr Nigel's office.

The outer office became very quiet with everyone aware that Bobby Douglas was just across the desk from Liz and June.

Five minutes later Sylvia marched out and went straight through to the drawing office, passing her younger sister, Fiona, as she responded to her own summons to Mr Nigel's room.

When she came out she was white-faced and near to tears, and made immediately for the cloakroom.

Liz wanted to go to her but held back since she wasn't supposed to know about the new plans that would affect Sylvia's and Fiona's jobs.

When she glanced up her eyes met Bobby's perplexed gaze.

'What's going on?' he hissed.

Liz shrugged. 'I haven't spoken to Mr Nigel this morning,' she answered truthfully.

Around mid-morning Will handed her a brown overall, to go down into the yard with him.

Once they were out of the office she had to walk quickly to keep up with him as they headed for the Loft, but there was something she wanted to say to him.

'Will,' she began tentatively, 'I think you should know that you might come up against . . . ' She stopped, searching for the right words.

'I'm sure there are some in the office, and in the yard, too, who think I shouldn't be chief cost clerk. But I'm not worried,' he finished dryly, without breaking his stride or glancing towards her, and her hackles rose at how he had dismissed her friendly warning.

Liz hardly noticed the noise of the engines being tested in the Experimental Shop, or the men up on stagings shouting instructions to those on the deck above.

Will was one of the few who had immediate access to the sensitive Loft area, with its priceless information on the exact specifications of the ships and their fittings. As they neared it, he nodded towards the ship on the slipway.

'Go and ask your father when her propellers could be fitted,' he directed.

Immediately Liz made for where Robbie was standing over a large, smooth metal plate with Archie Gilmour.

'Robbie! Here's bonnie lassie to see you,' Archie said with a grin. He'd known Liz since she was a child.

Liz asked about the propellers and carefully noted down the answer she was given.

Then Archie smiled and nodded beyond her.

'It looks as if someone else is anxious to speak to you.'

Liz froze. She knew at once it was Andy Knox.

Turning slowly she saw the tall, broad-shouldered figure making for her.

'Hello, Liz,' he called, but just as he reached her, an office-boy came running towards them.

'Miss Johnstone!' he blurted out. 'You've to come at once to the Loft, and bring your notebook. Mr Wingrave wants to see you.'

A call to the Loft was like a royal summons, and Liz gladly made her escape from Andy.

When she got to his office, Mr Wingrave welcomed her, holding a bone-china coffee pot and motioning her to a seat.

'Would you like to join us,' he asked, 'as we discuss business after the holiday?'

Liz glanced at Will, the only other person there, and felt her colour rise at the mischief in his expression. Was he behind this summons to get her away from the attentions of Andy Knox?

Mr Wingrave poured the coffee and began asking about the broken engagement, and, more surprisingly, about the relationship between Mr Nigel and Mrs Martin.

Liz answered carefully, uncertain in what capacity he was inquiring. Was it merely as an interested neighbour, or more seriously as a colleague of the managing director, who was also Mr Nigel's cousin?

Then suddenly his questions became more personal.

'And you're awaiting the return of

Keith Watson in a few weeks, aren't you?' he remarked, stirring his coffee. 'His father was saying the family may settle in Canada once the child is born.'

Liz sat rigid, desperate to ask who was included in the proposed move. Was it only Eddie Watson, his wife, Jean, and the child? Or was Keith involved, too? She couldn't help feeling that Mr Wingrave was somehow alerting her — though to what, exactly, she wasn't sure.

'That's news to me,' Liz said stiffly, taken by surprise. 'As far as I knew Mr Watson wanted his wife to come home after the baby was born.'

'I've encouraged him to think of Canada,' Mr Wingrave continued. 'A new start might be advantageous in the circumstances . . .'

The point was left hanging and it was a relief for Liz when the talk went on to more technical matters, and she took the usual notes. So much more straightforward than trying to make sense of tangled human relationships!

That afternoon, Liz was busy in Mr Nigel's room and was later than usual in finishing. She was alone as she closed up the office, and was startled when Andy Knox appeared in the doorway.

'You're a difficult girl to get by yourself.' He smiled and put an arm up making a barrier to her exit. 'There's a good picture on in the Rosevale tonight. Would you like to come with me?'

Liz panicked, but only for a moment. This was the moment she had been dreading all weekend — now she must be decisive. She collected herself and took a deep breath.

'I can't, Andy,' she said in a rush. 'I owe it to Keith. We have an understanding. He writes very regularly and his letters confirm his special feelings for me.'

He stared down at her, his features angry, and his arm fell from the doorway.

'Will Robertson told me as much today,' he growled, then swung away without another word.

Liz stood rooted for a moment, the colour draining from her face, but as she walked away she felt a certain pleasure. It seemed Will had got involved after all. She hoped that would end Andy's interest in her — but somehow she doubted it.

Robbie's Injured!

As August slipped into September and the trees began to change colour, Sylvia McDonald's broken engagement was consigned to history. In Burnham's office now, the interest centred on the new tracers' department where the two McDonald sisters worked in a spirit of non-cooperation. However, eventually they saw the error of their ways and after a friendly warning buckled down and seldom left their desks.

Liz was surprised when Sylvia stopped at her desk one afternoon.

'Wait for me at stopping time. I've got some news,' she said, and hurried away before Liz could say a word.

Liz had seen little of Sylvia since helping her to send back engagement presents and cancel wedding arrangements in the weeks after the Fair holiday.

Her eye caught Bobby Douglas's opposite, and he grinned at her, confirming that the news involved him, and as she speculated as to what it could be she knew she was glad of the diversion to stop her brooding over the scrappy letters arriving from Keith.

True, they came regularly enough, but they made boring reading. It was ages since she'd received one with lovely warming phrases about his feelings for her. But what concerned her even more was that he never mentioned anything about his family settling in Canada, as Mr Wingrave had told her. She wondered if Eddie Watson had misunderstood his son's plans.

'I'm glad you're alone and managed to dump that June Martin,' Sylvia said, linking her arm in Liz's as they met on their way out of the office.

'I didn't! June's . . . ' Liz started to defend her friend, but Sylvia was dismissive.

'I've nothing against her personally. It's just all these incomers. They can't have the same feeling for the place as people like us who've worked at Burnham's since we left school, and our fathers before us.' Sylvia smugly believed these sentiments as did the other traditionalists in the yard.

Sylvia's pettiness irritated Liz, but she'd had a tiring day, so her reply was measured.

'These incomers, as you call them, have brought skills and a breadth of experience to the firm that none of us 'born and bred' in Burnham's ever could have.'

'Oh, forget them.' Sylvia waved a haughty hand, then paused before dropping her voice to say almost primly in a whisper, 'Bobby and I have decided to get married this month!'

'But — but — Sylvia! You've only been courting for a few weeks! It's too quick,' Liz blurted out.

'No, it isn't!' Sylvia protested. 'Bobby wants us to get married. And we've taken on the rent of the flat. The factor allowed it — says I deserve some happiness after the tales Greg Scott has been spreading about me.'

Greg hadn't spared Sylvia in his criticism of the McDonald family and through it he'd succeeded in alienating a lot of people, so that it was generally accepted that the break had been a wise move on her part.

'But can you afford the flat on Bobby's wage?' Liz asked, practical to the core.

'My mother says I can work in the shop at dinner-time, when it's busiest,' Sylvia answered. 'Anyway, so much has changed with all these new methods the incomers have brought into Burnham's that I've lost interest.'

Liz wanted to point out that she had just claimed the good of the firm was embedded in her being but it would be lost on Sylvia now her mind was set on this course of action.

'Bobby and I want you to be our bridesmaid — and when Keith comes home, maybe you'd ask him to be the best man?'

Liz gaped, questions tumbling around in her brain, as she stuttered, 'But — but Keith hardly knows Bobby — Greg was his pal. Bobby's not even a close friend. And what about your sisters? Won't they expect to be bridesmaids? They were going to be the last time,' she couldn't resist adding.

'No. We're arranging this wedding on our own.'

They crossed Dumbarton Road and were making their way up the slope of Yarrowholm Street as Sylvia justified herself.

'It was really my idea to have Keith as best man, because I thought it would be nice for you — I mean, he'd be involved in the wedding preparations, just like you,' Sylvia encouraged.

At once Liz heard alarm bells ring as she realised Sylvia was trying to manipulate her. She suspected that in fact Sylvia wanted her to do the organising.

She surprised herself by saying in an even tone, 'What do you mean, 'involved'? I thought you said you were arranging this yourselves?'

As they turned into their close and started up the stairs Liz was thinking on her feet.

'I hope you're not counting on me to be a lot of help. I've already promised old Mrs Cunningham that I'll help out on a couple of weekends soon with some charity coffee mornings that are coming up. And as for Keith, he's never been a best man before.'

'Well, you must try to persuade him,' Sylvia pleaded urgently.

'But why Keith?' Liz was at a loss.

'Because Andy Knox is Bobby's best friend and it could be awkward if he was best man.'

* * *

It was almost ten o'clock in the morning and although it was only mid-September, the lights were on in Burnham's office. Outside it was dull and drizzly, the clouds almost touching the chimney pots of the surrounding tenements.

The depressing weather had no effect on Liz, sitting with her head down at her high Victorian desk, calculating Burnham's weekly balance. Little thrills of excitement coursed through her at the thought of Keith's homecoming the next day.

She'd heard from his father earlier in the week that his ship, the Turnbull, was docking at Yorkhill Quay on Saturday afternoon, and the previous night she'd re-read all the beautiful words of affection he'd written when he'd set off for Canada.

'What should we wear this evening?' June's whisper over the desk interrupted Liz's thoughts.

She had to drag her mind away from thoughts of Keith to focus on preparing the Assembly Rooms for Mrs Cunningham's charity coffee morning the next day. She didn't want to let Will's grandmother down.

'Not slacks! The committee ladies

might not approve!' she warned.

'Bring a pinny to put over what you're wearing now. That's what I'm doing.'

'It's a pity we work on a Saturday morning. We'll miss the coffee morning itself tomorrow.'

Liz smiled and returned to the ledgers, glad that June was looking forward to helping out. There would be quite a squad of them with Andrew, the twins Frank and Jim, and Fiona and Lindsey McDonald from across the landing. Only Sylvia would be missing. She and Bobby were busy decorating their flat ahead of their wedding in a couple of weeks.

Just then, Will stopped at her desk, holding out a brown linen overall, and Liz felt a flicker of annoyance. They didn't usually go down to the yard on a Friday afternoon.

'Sorry,' Will said when he saw her frown. 'There's been a change to the design of the propeller shaft so we need to visit the Loft again and see your father.'

'I could do the balance for you,' June offered.

Liz pondered, then smiled.

'Why not? You've got to learn.'

She slipped into the brown coat, lifted her notebook and followed Will out.

The rain was now a steady downpour, and the wind gusting off the river drove it into their faces. Liz was glad to shelter under Will's large umbrella as they walked towards the Loft at the other end of the yard.

'Your father must be frozen working in this weather,' Will murmured, the concern in his voice surprising her.

'My mother'll have a change of clothes waiting for him at dinner-time,' Liz answered, and guiltily realised as the rain stung her face how she took for granted that her father worked on in all weathers. She even accepted as normal her mother preparing thick sheets of brown paper to go under his shirt front for warmth.

As they neared the platers' shed, Liz

became aware of a group of men milling around, some keeping the rain off with canvas sacking around their shoulders.

Liz registered that something was wrong when Will thrust the umbrella into her hands and ran ahead.

As the crowd of men parted to let him through, she glimpsed a figure on the ground, half-buried under a metal plate, and knew at once it was her father.

'Dad!' she cried in fear and ran forward.

She knelt down and sheltered her father's head and shoulders under the umbrella, flinching as he winced and groaned as the men gently lifted the heavy metal plate off him.

'Just a flesh wound,' he whispered through clenched teeth. 'The ambulance-room will put a dressing on and I'll be all right . . . '

Two of the men helped him to his feet, ready to take him to the ambulance-room, but Will stepped forward.

'No. He'll never make it.' He glanced quickly around. 'Fetch that board — we'll use it as a stretcher . . . '

Within moments he had supervised Robbie's transfer to the board, which was grasped by six pairs of hands.

Heads down, the wind whipping against their clothes, the men carried him steadily to the ambulance-room. Liz kept up with them, holding the umbrella over her father's head.

Sister McBride was at the ready, and shooed out those no longer needed, including Andy Knox. He glared at Will, who was allowed to stay.

Liz met Sister McBride's eye and stood her ground.

The pervasive smell of the medical room made her feel queasy, but Will's solid presence beside her was comforting.

Robbie regained consciousness when the nursing sister had cleaned up the wound. Immediately he tried to sit up but she pressed him back.

'Will you please lie still, Mr Johnstone!' she ordered.

She turned to one of the helpers still in the room.

'What happened?'

'We were lifting the plate,' he explained, 'when two of us slipped and it fell on Robbie.'

Sister McBride nodded.

'It's not as bad as I first thought, but we could do with an ambulance — '

'No! I'm not going to the infirmary,' Robbie interrupted. 'I've got a son who's a doctor.'

Sister McBride hesitated, then she nodded.

Her father also worked in the shipyards, and she knew what a stay in the infirmary could mean. Often the injured man came out to no job, especially if the current ship was nearly finished, as was this one.

Will sensed her hesitation.

'I've got a car,' he offered quickly. 'I can run him home.'

Liz felt a rush of relief as he took Sister McBride's silence as agreement and hurried out.

'But you realise I'll have to mention in my report that you signed yourself out,' Sister McBride warned Robbie.

In a few minutes Will was back.

'I've brought the car to the side door.'

'Is it suitable for conveying an injured man?' Sister McBride queried and went to look out of the window.

She drew in her breath when she saw the sleek Riley Nine sports car.

'That looks like a very expensive car for a cost clerk,' she observed.

'I bought it second-hand. A real bargain,' Will said slightly defensively.

'It's easy seen you're a bachelor!' Sister McBride sniffed, then amazed him by insisting on covering the seats to prevent the men's oily clothes marking them.

Sister's comments weren't lost on Liz. As she made her way back to the office, she began to wonder what Will was like away from work.

★ ★ ★

239

Esther Johnstone glanced up at the clock. The fish pie was ready for the oven at dinner-time and she must do a baking before then, for Will Robertson was coming to tea.

But first there were the door brasses. Normally she'd have done them an hour ago, but she was avoiding Olive McDonald next door. She'd heard enough about Sylvia's broken engagement . . .

But Olive would be at the shop by now, Esther calculated — wrongly, as it turned out, for a few moments later, as she was rubbing up the letter-box, the door opposite opened.

'You're late this morning, Esther,' Olive observed cheerfully as she shut the door behind her.

Esther inwardly sighed with relief as she recognised Olive's more expansive mood.

'I never thought I'd say it, but our Sylvia's engagement to Bobby Douglas is the wisest move she's ever made. He's transforming their flat, and he's done all my little repairs in the house and the shop.'

Esther nodded, marvelling that Olive could talk now as if she'd always approved of her daughter's change of heart.

'And I'm relieved everything's worked out well for Jean Watson, too!' Olive sighed happily. 'She's had a little boy. Haven't you heard?' she added when she saw Esther's puzzled face.

Esther shook her head.

'Who told you?' she asked.

'Eddie Watson, when I met him this morning. He said the baby came last week. He must've got a telegram . . .'

Just then the sound of heavy footsteps and men's voices echoed in the stairwell.

Olive peered over the banister and stifled a cry.

'It's your Robbie! He's been hurt!'

Esther dashed out to look as Will Robertson bounded up the stairs, his hair plastered to his head with the rain.

'There's been an accident,' Will

explained. 'A plate fell on him and gashed his leg. Maybe Andrew could stitch it up? He didn't want to go to the infirmary.'

Two men carried Robbie up the last stairs, and the sudden shock of seeing her husband in this condition made Esther feel quite faint for a moment.

Seeing her pallor, Olive grasped her arm and led her into the house just as Andrew appeared in his pyjamas. He had been sleeping after being called out to an emergency during the night but this commotion had wakened him.

Esther sank into the chair and watched as Olive lifted the ever-simmering kettle to sterilise the medical instruments Andrew had put in a bowl.

It was chastening to see Olive carrying out the tasks that by right she should be doing — especially after the way she'd criticised her neighbour recently.

But she watched with pride, too, as Andrew calmly and expertly tended to his father.

Once he was satisfied there was nothing more he could do, Esther and Olive prepared Robbie for bed, then saw the men out. But even in her anxiety about her husband, Esther was aware of another nagging worry. They would be without a wage while Robbie was unable to work . . .

'Esther,' Olive said decisively, 'your family can come over to my house at dinner-time. You've got it all ready — I'll just put it in my oven. It'll give Robbie a bit of peace, and you a break.' She paused, and gave a sad little smile. 'My Peter loved peace and quiet when he was in pain.'

She went to the table and lifted the large ashet, domed with mashed potato, which was waiting for the oven. Then she bustled out, brushing aside Esther's thanks at the door.

'It's the least I can do, Esther. You've been a good friend to me, always ready to listen, when there's many who couldn't be bothered with me and my troubles.'

With that, she crossed the landing to open her door, leaving Esther feeling ashamed of her earlier thoughts.

At that point, Will, who had remained quietly in the background, made to leave.

'I'm very grateful for what you've done, Will,' Esther said hoarsely.

'It's the least I could do. But look — I won't come for tea tonight,' he told her gently. 'But maybe I could take Liz straight to the Assembly Rooms, and we'll have a bite to eat on our way?'

'That would be best,' she agreed, happy to encourage Liz to be with him.

'That Will Robertson's a fine lad,' Robbie whispered drowsily from the bed, his eyes already closing from the sedative Andrew had given him. 'He'd make a good son-in-law!'

Esther gave a small sigh. She and Will's grandmother felt exactly the same. Only Liz seemed to have other ideas.

She had watched her daughter go off to work that morning excited and buoyed-up with the thought of seeing Keith the next day. She'd apparently forgotten the disappointment of their few dates together — or was ignoring them, unwilling to admit to herself that Keith might not live up to her dreams of him.

Andrew returned to the kitchen, putting on his coat, ready for late surgery.

'How long will he be off work?' Esther asked in an undertone.

'A fortnight at least.'

Esther nodded and sighed. Two weeks without the wages of the main earner was a blow, especially after their holiday.

Still, it wasn't so bad. Thankfully Andrew was now contributing from what he earned as a trainee GP, and the twins were into their fifth-year apprenticeship. And Harry, too, would be able to give her something, while Liz was always generous.

'At least with a doctor in the house,' Andrew said, as if reading her thoughts, 'you'll not have extra medical bills!' He smiled, pulling cycle clips from his pocket. 'I'll see you at tea-time. And don't worry — he's going to be all right.'

Robbie was peacefully asleep by now, so she went through to the big room and watched from the oriel window as Andrew, his black doctor's bag strapped on behind the saddle, rode down the slope of Yarrowholm Street.

In a year or two he hoped to buy a motor-car to do his rounds.

Esther closed her eyes and offered a little prayer that health and strength in the family would allow it.

★ ★ ★

The finishing horns of all the shipyards were sounding out their different tones as Will hurried Liz along to a side street where his car was parked.

'I'm so grateful for your help, Will. My father . . . '

'Don't thank me. I feel I'm just

246

repaying a debt,' he replied. 'He's one of the few who's treated me decently since I came to Burnham's. I've even heard him defending me to some who resent my promotion — especially to your friend Andy Knox.'

Liz bristled. 'Andy's just a boy who was at school with me,' she said sharply.

'He lets everyone know he wants to be more than that,' Will commented, his eyes firmly on the road ahead as he drove.

'Well, he's got no right!' Liz said heatedly, colour rising in her cheeks. 'Andy's a fine young man in his own way. He's supported his family from an early age. But I've given him no encouragement.'

She was about to continue at length, but noticed that Will was smiling.

'I like to hear you when you're riled!' he commented. 'It's the nearest you get to being bad-tempered.'

Her exasperation with him quickly changed to bewilderment as he stopped the car outside his grandparents' villa.

'We may as well have our tea here,' he told her. 'There's stuff my grandmother wants taken to the Assembly Rooms. And she wants to come along later, too. She has an interview arranged with your Harry.'

'But I can't possibly . . . ' Liz began, wishing she was wearing the good clothes she'd laid out for meeting Keith.

'My grandmother told me to bring you when she heard about your dad. It's her way of helping your mother. They became good friends when they met during the holidays.'

Will took her elbow and led her into the wide, carpeted hall.

'We're through here,' Mrs Cunningham's voice trilled from a cosy room at the end of the hall.

There a table covered with a starched white cloth was set for four, with shining cutlery and pretty dishes.

'Come autumn, this is the only warm, draught-free room in the house,' the old lady explained. 'And my dear husband says I hibernate here from September to the end of March.'

She welcomed Liz with a kiss on the cheek, and beckoned her to a seat beside the blazing fire.

She saw Liz's glance rest on the photographs of a young woman on the mantelpiece, and smiled.

'That's Amy. My daughter . . . Will's mother,' she said softly. 'Those were taken when she was just seventeen. Just before she went to art school.'

She lifted one down and sighed. 'She was so high spirited and self willed — we probably spoiled her. Consumption claimed both her and her husband when Will was just sixteen.'

She replaced the pictures as her husband came in.

'You know, my dear, I'm shockingly neglected,' he told Liz with a smile. 'All my wife's attentions are given to her charities. If it was another man, I'd know what to do, but how to combat committees of ladies is beyond me.'

Liz laughed, for the look that went

between the two elderly people told of a love tested by time and trials. But, at the back of her mind, she did wonder why all the photographs in the room were of Will's mother. She felt it was strange that there were none of his father, or even of Will as a child.

★ ★ ★

All too soon it was time to leave the Cunninghams' fireside and head into town.

In the Assembly Rooms that evening, the twins were subdued as they helped carry in tables for the next day's coffee morning. Even the normally ebullient Harry was quiet when he arrived from the newspaper office.

It was the first time any of the family had seen Robbie ill and in bed.

Mrs Cunningham noted the concern of all the young Johnstones, and she understood their anxiety.

However, Harry did his best to sound cheerful as he spoke to her, his reporter's notebook and pencil poised at the ready.

'I'm here to do my first interview,' he announced. 'The editor's allowed me out.'

She took him into a small office and gave him a very full interview on their work for needy children, and at the end of it Harry's eyes shone with gratitude — she had given him enough for several articles.

Once Harry had left her, Mrs Cunningham went to look for Liz, and when she found her she stood watching her for a few moments, admiring her neat, graceful movements. She was a girl any mother would be glad to see her son — or grandson — marry!

Liz was unaware of the scrutiny, her thoughts on her reunion with Keith.

'I'm glad to get you on your own.' June interrupted Liz's thoughts as they got out more tablecloths. 'I've got some news, but keep it quiet.'

June paused, quickly checking that no-one else could hear, then announced, 'My mother and Nippy Nigel are getting engaged tomorrow!'

'That's nice,' Liz replied. 'But if he's to be your stepfather, you'll have to stop calling him Nippy Nigel! How do you feel about it?'

'I'm pleased.' June nodded. 'Especially as Mummy's got what she wanted. Mr Burnham senior has asked her to continue as his secretary.'

Liz gasped in surprised.

'You mean after she's married?'

June nodded. 'He even told them not to delay their engagement since the yard is seething with rumours of their intentions.'

Liz wondered how much of this came from her conversation with Mr Wingrave in the office.

'Nigel's housekeeper is to stay on and look after the domestic side of things, which suits Mummy beautifully,' June continued cheerfully.

'Will you be going to live in Kirn?' This was where Nigel Burnham had his home.

'No, I'll keep on the Yarrowholm Street flat.'

'You mean — live by yourself?'

June laughed at the amazement on Liz's face.

'Yes! After all, I am twenty!'

Liz tried to disguise her surprise. In Yarrowholm Street, girls always stayed with their parents and only left home to get married.

Lindsey, the youngest McDonald sister, approached just then, trying not to look flustered.

'Liz, will you have a word with Fiona? She's upset some of the committee ladies. In her eyes, no-one's doing anything properly except her!'

Liz looked over and could see Fiona confronting Jim and Frank. The twins looked ready to mutiny, and she groaned inwardly.

'These two are going at a snail's pace bringing up the chairs. I could do better myself,' Fiona stormed when Liz went over.

'If you feel like that we'll take over

and the boys can help set up the last of the tables,' Liz suggested quietly, and pointed the twins to the other end of the hall.

'No sooner said than done!' Frank and Jim didn't need a second telling, and hurried off to join the other men.

Fiona sat down, unexpectedly limp and deflated.

'Fiona, what's wrong?' Liz asked.

'Oh, I don't know. It's just that everything's gone wrong recently.'

'You have had a few disappointments in the past few months,' Liz reflected.

'It's so disheartening seeing someone else in charge of the tracers,' Fiona continued miserably. 'But what really gets me is that the new woman does it better than either Sylvia or me.'

Liz smiled and nodded, recalling her own similar experience.

'I felt the same way when Eleanor Martin got the secretary's job. Then I discovered that compared to her I was only an amateur.'

How desperately she'd wanted that

position, Liz remembered.

'At least you got some promotion,' Fiona put in, 'helping Will Robertson down in the yard. But I'm still doing the same work and, what's worse, I've realised I'm not as competent as I thought.'

Fiona let out a long sigh.

'And it doesn't seem fair that Sylvia's on to her second fiancé. And you've got Keith and Andy Knox *and* Will Robertson all in tow. I've just wanted the one — your brother Andrew.' Fiona looked thoroughly dejected as she continued, 'But now he's spending all his time with June Martin — he doesn't even seem to notice me now.'

Liz gasped. 'But you've had plenty of boys who've been sweet on you!'

Fiona had never been short of boyfriends, and had made no secret of the fact that it was only once Andrew was no longer a penniless student that she would turn her attention to him!

Liz remembered wondering how her neighbour managed to go out with so many boys while insisting that she still carried a torch for Andrew. However, she decided to say nothing about that, though she felt obliged to put Fiona in the picture as far as her own affairs were concerned.

'It's common knowledge that Andy Knox is just looking for a wife now that he's been made a charge-hand. And as for Will Robertson — he's certainly not interested in me in that way. He does nothing but tease me.'

As Liz made no mention of Keith, Fiona drew her own conclusion.

'Well, if Keith's the one you want, why are you here when he's just arrived home after being at sea for months?' Fiona asked sullenly.

'He's not due home till tomorrow afternoon,' Liz replied evenly.

'Well, it must have been a ghost I met on the stairs on my way here.'

Facing Keith

On the journey home from the Assembly Rooms, Liz sat silently in the front seat of the car with Will. No-one noticed how quiet she was, for there was high-spirited hilarity from the back seat.

The twins, Jim and Frank, and two of the McDonald sisters were squashed together. Fiona McDonald was being especially witty, trying to make up for the shock she knew she had given Liz.

'Come up for some tea and scones. Dad would enjoy a chat with you,' Jim invited Will as the car stopped at the close.

Will consulted his watch.

'Why not? It's barely half-past nine.'

He looked around for some encouragement from Liz, but she was yearning to be alone with her thoughts. Keith was home — and he hadn't got in touch with her.

Wearily she climbed the stairs, hurt and bewildered. Why had Keith slipped back home unannounced? Why hadn't he contacted her straightaway? Hadn't he been counting the days to their reunion the way she had?

Liz's heart was chilled and her footsteps were heavy at the tail-end of the little group.

'Hello, Liz!'

At first she couldn't believe her ears, and was astonished to see Keith, tanned and smiling, at the open door of his home. He moved forward and gave her a brotherly hug.

'Come in. We've been listening for you.' He drew her over the threshold. 'See you later,' he called over his shoulder to the others and closed the door.

Liz was in a sudden haze of happiness, aware of Keith's arm around her waist as he guided her inside. However, the sight of Mr Watson sitting by the ash-strewn hearth blunted her pleasure. She resented him sharing her first meeting with Keith.

'Sit down.' Mr Watson pointed at a chair with the stem of his pipe. 'We were just talking about you and all your fine certificates for typing, shorthand and book-keeping.'

Keith nodded proudly. 'I told Dad you could manage the office of any business.'

'Well, thank you,' she said, puzzled.

'They'll certainly be an asset to our plans,' Mr Watson replied smugly.

'Plans? What plans?'

'We'll get to that later.' Keith changed the subject abruptly. 'I've so much to tell you about my trip.'

He started describing the Turnbull's voyage and didn't spare her the technical details, unaware as her gaze strayed to idle round the room.

Liz couldn't help noticing the way the men's jackets and pullovers were draped over the backs of chairs — the room was very untidy.

It was all so different from her own home immediately above, where everything was neat and clean.

'Ay!' Mr Watson growled, seeing her gaze. 'It's a mess since those daughters of mine refused to come back. But now you're walking out with our Keith, you could tidy the place up a bit and do our washing.'

If Keith was embarrassed, he said nothing, while Liz couldn't believe what she was hearing. For a moment she could hardly speak. When she did, she struggled to keep her voice controlled.

'I don't think that will be possible,' she said. 'My first duty is to my mother since my father's been injured. In fact, I'm afraid I have to go now.'

Keith nodded that he understood, and took her to the door, where he stood awkwardly looking down at her.

'That was a strange conversation.' Liz tried to sound reasonable. 'What was all that about my qualifications?'

'Oh, nothing. Just talk . . . you know.' Keith shrugged, then he pulled her into his arms and was kissing her passionately.

'That's how we should have started,' he said when he raised his head. 'It's great to see you again. I'd forgotten how pretty you are.'

'Pretty?' Liz laughed. She was delighted to hear him saying it, yet too honest with herself to believe it. 'I thought you saw me as neat and sensible. The girl next door.'

'No. To me you're beautiful and with a good head on your shoulders. And from what I hear, I'm not alone. Andy Knox and Will Robertson would like what I have in my arms at this moment.'

As his arms tightened around her and he kissed her again, Liz suddenly wanted to be free.

This wasn't the same Keith who had left in May. They'd only had a few dates together by then, and in any case, he'd been so distracted about his mother's sudden departure that they'd hardly talked, never mind kissed.

She pushed him away.

'How was your mother when you saw her?' she asked a little breathlessly.

'Mum?' Keith was taken aback. 'Oh, she's very happy. Her widowed brother and his family are very grateful for all she's done for them. She won't come back here, so my father's decided to go to Canada and we're . . . '

He stopped himself, then quickly switched to Sylvia McDonald's broken engagement.

'It was a big shock to hear about Greg and Sylvia. While I was away I'd thought we could announce our engagement at their wedding.'

Liz was open-mouthed at this casual mention of getting engaged. It was the first time such a thing had been discussed. But she didn't want to jeopardise anything between them and kept her tone light.

'Don't you think you're taking things a little fast, Keith?' She tried to smile. 'I mean, you haven't even asked me to marry you yet. And a decision like that needs some thought.'

'Oh, don't come over all coy, Liz. We've known each other all our lives. There's nothing more to know — unless you've got some fancy ideas about working in Burnham's. I hear you've been gadding about the yard with the high and mighty Will Robertson.'

'Keith, since you've known me all your life, you should realise 'gadding about' is the last thing I'd do,' she answered sharply.

He took a deep breath and nodded, a little shamefaced.

'Sorry. I can't help being jealous.'

He took her hands gently in his and smiled appealingly, a lock of hair flopping endearingly over his tanned forehead.

Her heart did a little somersault. This was more like she'd dreamed their reunion would be. She smiled.

'You don't have to worry about Will being interested in me in that way. We work together. That's all.'

They heard the door above open and as Will came running downstairs Keith quickly put a possessive arm about Liz's shoulder and pulled her close.

She felt awkward when, his eyes glinting with amusement at the calculated move, Will stopped and extended his hand to Keith.

'I'm Will Robertson, and you'll be Keith. Liz'll be delighted to see you home. She had her glad rags all laid out for tomorrow.' With that he nodded and continued on down the stairs.

'Your father told me the Turnbull was docking tomorrow afternoon, so everyone in the office knew,' Liz explained when they were alone again.

'We had the tides and wind in our favour, so we berthed quicker than expected,' Keith said airily, and swept her back into his arms again, his lips crushing hers.

'Keith!' she gasped. 'I'm not quite used to this yet.' Pushing him away, she continued, 'And now I must get upstairs to see how my father is.'

'I've got five months of kisses to make up,' Keith said ruefully, releasing her with a show of reluctance.

Liz stumbled upstairs, her heart pounding alarmingly, and waited for a few moments until she heard him close the door.

She took a powder compact from her handbag and checked her appearance, but before she could knock at her own door it suddenly opened and her mother stepped out.

'I didn't want you ringing the bell. Olive McDonald's here helping Andrew change your dad's dressings. Best wait till the morning to see him. He's nearly asleep now.'

Esther followed Liz through to her bedroom, glad of the chance to have a minute or two with her daughter at the end of a very trying day.

'I'm glad you've met up with Keith at last,' she remarked, 'though I'm surprised he wasn't in touch with you sooner. Did you know he's been home since last night?'

'The wind and tide were with them, he said,' Liz answered evenly, disguising the fact that he'd arrived home even earlier than he'd led her to believe.

'It seems strange that you're about the last to meet him. He and his father were over at the Wingraves' last night. Apparently they've decided to call the new baby Nathan Wingrave Watson — I wonder why?' Esther ended dryly.

She was suspicious of Eddie Watson's motives. He always had his eye on the main chance and knew that Nathan Wingrave had an influential position in the shipyard.

* * *

Next morning, after a fitful night's sleep, Liz's thoughts were muddled. She was still disappointed that Keith hadn't made seeing her his first priority — despite having marriage in mind.

That was unexpected, too. They'd never discussed a life together, even light-heartedly, on those few dates

266

they'd had before he went to Canada. Of course, then he'd been preoccupied with his mother's sudden departure, but talk of marriage was definitely not what she'd expected. Not for a long time.

When she arrived at Burnham's, the atmosphere was strangely tense although usually the Saturday half-day was relaxed and easy-going.

Today, Mr Burnham, Mr Nigel and the chief draughtsman were in the Private Room, already in conference. Eleanor Martin was busy taking files and job cost sheets to them.

The chief draughtsman came out and returned with rolls of drawings, and then Mr Nigel took in special bank files from the locked safe.

'Something awful's happened,' June Martin whispered. 'Nippy Nigel came and got us out of bed around seven this morning to whisk Mummy into the office. Some firm has gone bankrupt or something,' she continued when she saw Liz's puzzled expression. 'Not the best day to announce an engagement either,' she added with a little grimace.

Liz gulped, immediately thinking of last night's conversation with Keith. But then she quickly realised that of course June was talking about her mother and Mr Nigel's plans.

The two girls got their heads down and turned their attention to their columns of figures, although it was difficult with so many distractions. Everyone in the commercial office watched, subdued, as different foremen came up to the office, their faces grim.

At last Bobby Douglas returned from the Private Room to his seat opposite June and Liz and groaned as he slumped down, his head in his hands.

'It couldn't have come at a worse time. A week today I'm supposed to get married. I could be unemployed by then!' He raised a miserable face, and gave a deep sigh.

'The company which ordered the Two-seven-two has gone bankrupt, with a load of money outstanding. It'll probably mean job losses. Burnham's will have to fight to stay afloat.'

June turned questioning eyes to Liz who explained quietly, 'They usually prune the office staff to the bone when things get difficult . . . It'll be like when I started ten years ago as an office girl. There were only four here then.'

Just then, Will came out of the Private Room and went to the costing desk under the window. He sat frowning for several minutes at the papers there, then he turned to Liz.

'Bring your notebook. We have to go down to the yard.'

She took the brown overall he offered her and they made for the swing door together.

It was the first time Liz had wished that Will would tease her. She'd never known him to look so grim.

In the yard, the wall of noise which always greeted her was as loud as ever, and the arcs of red-hot rivets flashed high on the stagings as usual. But little groups of men were clustered, having discussions, their faces betraying their concern.

Will sighed. 'News travels fast!'

'So it's true what Bobby told us about the Two-seven-two?' Liz asked.

'Yes, I'm afraid so.'

Andy Knox's tall, red-spattered figure suddenly confronted them. For once, his eyes were not on Liz.

'What's the latest?' he asked. 'Everyone's wondering what's going on.'

'If we can line up a new buyer, and fix an agreement with the bank to tide us over, we'll be OK.' Will's tone was cautious. 'But it's a big 'if'.'

'How long will that take?'

Will shrugged. 'The news of the bankruptcy only broke late yesterday. Mr Burnham has been in the office since half past six this morning.'

Andy sighed wearily.

'Lithgow's up the river had ships left on their hands. It took over three years to sell them.' He looked gloomy as he recalled the hardships that time had brought. Then, in a change of mood, he touched his cap to them both.

'Anyway, thanks for keeping me in the picture.' And with that he was away.

'Strange how adversity brings out the best,' Will said. 'That's the first time the red-leaders' gaffer has given me a civil word.'

Then, in an undertone he added, 'Mind, he's only recently got promotion, so he'll be a prime target for cuts.' Silently they walked towards the Loft.

As they were passing the platers' shed, Archie Gilmour called to Liz to ask how her father was doing after his accident.

'He slept well enough, and Andrew's pleased that there's no fever. Mrs McDonald, our neighbour across the landing, has nursing experience, and she's helping him change the dressings,' Liz replied, touched by his concern.

'I hope he's better soon. I just hope he's still got a job to come back to.'

Will and Liz made their way along to Mr Wingrave's office at the end of the Loft. It overlooked the long, smooth, ballroom-like floor which was covered with chalked shapes of ships' components.

Mr Wingrave stood up, shaking his head sadly as they came in.

'Morning, Will.' He gestured through the glass to the chalk drawings. 'You'll be wanting me to estimate how few men could do this work.'

Liz stood quietly beside the two men as they looked down on the expanse of floor, their eyes travelling frequently to drawings on Mr Wingrave's desk.

He and Will discussed figures and man-hours, as well as mechanical details. Will had an amazing knowledge. He could turn his attention from minute technical specifications to details concerning costing to the last penny. Old Mr Standish, Will's predecessor, for all his fifty years of service with the firm, had never had such expertise.

They'd been busy for almost an hour when Mr Wingrave decided on a break.

Liz was enjoying the milky coffee from his bone china cups when she heard Will's sharp of intake of breath.

'Oh, no!' he groaned.

She followed his gaze to the group of men entering the Loft. The only person she didn't recognise was an elderly, bearded man wearing a long overcoat. His thick grey hair curled round the brim of his high-crowned bowler hat.

'Wait here and finish your coffee,' Mr Wingrave said as he got up to greet them, unaware of the tension the stranger had caused.

Liz glanced at Will's pale face.

'You look as if you've seen a ghost!'

'No. Just Sir Erwin Roderick McAllister — my grandfather — my father's father. It's the first time I've met him.'

Will almost spat out the words, then sat down with his back to the window, as if he couldn't bear to see more.

Mr Wingrave was breathless when he came in from meeting the new arrivals.

'Will, there's a gentleman here wants to meet you.'

'The desire isn't mutual,' Will said

273

through clenched teeth. 'I have no wish to meet him!'

Mr Wingrave stared at him for a few long moments as he gathered his thoughts.

'He's the chairman of the bank. Your feelings are of little importance when there are men in this yard whose jobs depend on his help,' Mr Wingrave said quietly but with stern authority. 'We need this man's goodwill to survive.'

Liz had only ever known Mr Wingrave as an affable old gentleman or courteous neighbour and was surprised at his tone. Now she tensely watched Will's reaction.

The gravity of the situation reached Will and, dropping his challenging expression, he rose from his chair and went out to meet the little group studying the drawings on the floor.

Liz and Mr Wingrave watched through the window.

'I'm afraid that was a bit of a test,' he murmured to her. 'At last, although Will has no desire to meet his grandfather, we now know he has a proper sense of loyalty to Burnham's.'

Liz frowned. She hadn't expected Mr Wingrave to be so calculating.

She was also mystified about Will's past. He never spoke of his parents, or his life before he had come to Burnham's. And last night, his grandmother had shown Liz pictures of his mother, but none of his father.

She'd thought it strange then, and now she was intrigued by Will's reaction to meeting his grandfather. Why had they never met before?

Mr Wingrave motioned her to sit down in the seat Will had just vacated. She would rather have watched the group from her previous place, but she knew better than to suggest otherwise.

As Mr Wingrave gave a little cough and adjusted his cuffs, Liz gave him her full attention.

'Talking of priorities — ' He paused, a little uncertain how to continue. 'Has Keith Watson contacted you yet?'

'We met up last night,' Liz told him,

uncertain where this was leading.

'Last night?' He looked at her in astonishment. 'But he came over to see Miss Agatha and myself the previous evening with his father. I'd have thought it would have been the other way about.'

He was echoing what her mother had said and all at once she didn't want to listen. She wanted to think about Keith's proposal, unromantic as it was, and enjoy knowing that he wanted to marry her. It had been her dream since they were at school. For so long it had been part of her, and she didn't want the dream spoiled.

Mr Wingrave broke into her thoughts. 'I told Keith he was fortunate to have a girl like you waiting for him, with all your qualifications and the ability to run any business.' He paused in distaste. 'I told him about the other young men wishing they were in his shoes.' He sniffed. 'I think it gave him some food for thought.'

'He Just Won't Listen!'

A week after his accident, Robbie was back in bed, after being up for most of the day. Now his breathing was regular, as he slept in the kitchen set-in bed.

The sound was reassuring to Esther as she dozed in her chair by the fire. It was Friday night and the rest of the family were all out.

Robbie was healing well and hoped to be fit for work in a week or two. There was a great wave of relief in Yarrowholm Street, for it looked as if there would be work for everyone. No-one was to be laid off at Burnham's, despite the crash of the Two-seven-two's buyer.

Esther jerked into wakefulness as the front door closed and Liz tiptoed into the kitchen. The older woman glanced at the clock in surprise. It was only ten o'clock. She was sure Liz and Keith had planned to have supper after the theatre.

Seeing her mother's expression, Liz paused on her way to her room.

'We've had a disagreement,' Liz said in explanation as she sank into her father's big chair.

Esther didn't speak, ashamed of her satisfaction at the news.

'Keith and his father want to emigrate to Canada,' Liz confided. 'Keith's uncle has property on the banks of one of the great lakes. They're planning to join him and set up a boat repair yard. In the summer, steam and sailing yachts come from Detroit and other cities in the States, and often need repairs.'

Esther concealed her growing concern as Liz described the plans Keith had for the future. At last she interrupted.

'So he wants you to marry him and go out to Canada and take on the office side of this business they're going to set up. Are you sure . . . ?'

'It's all right, Mum. I told him I'm not going. That's what we disagreed about.'

Esther was surprised at the dull finality in Liz's voice.

'And what did he have to say about that?'

Liz paused, recalling how incredulous he'd been.

'Well, he wasn't too pleased. He wanted to go and tell his father about it right away. So we didn't go for supper — we just came home.'

The deep sadness on her face hurt Esther.

There was a long silence between them as Liz sat staring into the fire, watching the fading embers.

She shivered as she recalled her delight at receiving Keith's letters; the beautiful phrases of love and affection had seemed to confirm everything she'd ever wished for.

Now those same words which she knew by heart rang hollow. She'd been shocked when Keith had confessed that they'd been written by a ship-mate. He'd tried to make light of it, insisting the sentiments were true and that he'd only enlisted the help of a friend because he wasn't very good with words and wanted to impress her.

Despite all his protestations, however, she knew with a blinding clarity that the words hadn't come from the heart and that she could never marry him now.

Esther waited in sympathetic silence, sensing the painful thoughts going through her daughter's mind.

Finally she said quietly, 'You're remembering it's Sylvia's wedding tomorrow, Liz? You'll not let this put a damper on things, will you? I feel we owe such a lot to her mother. Olive's been such a great help to Andrew. He and your dad both say she's a born nurse.'

'No, Mum — ' Liz smiled faintly. 'Keith and I are ready to be best man and bridesmaid as promised.'

She stood up to go to her room, dangerously close to tears.

'After the wedding reception, I'll finish things completely,' she said quietly. 'I want Keith to realise there's nothing between us.'

She sighed. 'The worst thing, Mum, is that there never really was anything more than my dreams — and his plans to make use of me in Canada.'

To Esther it was good news. Keith was a fine enough young man in his own way and she supposed he meant well, but she'd always felt he was been taking Liz's affection for granted, and she wanted more than that for her only daughter.

She smiled and tried to lighten the mood as a plan began to form in her mind.

'I'm glad Fiona and Lindsey McDonald have come to their senses at last,' she said quietly.

Liz looked up.

'What do you mean — come to their senses?'

'Well, they've decided to be Sylvia's bridesmaids after all. I think they must

281

have forgiven her for marrying Bobby instead of Greg,' Esther explained.

For the first time that evening, Liz smiled.

'Does that mean — I wouldn't have to be a bridesmaid?' she asked hopefully.

Liz had never wanted to take the place of Sylvia's sisters, and her own mother and Sylvia's both realised just how uncomfortable she felt about it. The sisters' change of heart surely meant she could now go to the wedding as an ordinary guest.

'Yes, I think it does,' Esther replied, 'and it might help ease a very embarrassing situation all round.'

She knew Liz wouldn't be looking forward to spending the day as a bridesmaid with Keith as the best man, and she was quite sure Olive and Sylvia would understand.

Esther got up to put the kettle on the hob for a late-night cup of tea with Olive, who usually popped across the landing about this time for a chat.

However, when the front doorbell jangled just then, she knew it couldn't be Olive — she never rang; she knew the door was always open.

Liz and Esther exchanged mystified looks, and the same thought struck both women as Liz went to answer the door.

As they'd expected, it was Keith, standing on the doorstep, frowning.

To allow Liz some privacy, Esther hastily crossed the landing to Olive McDonald's to give the McDonald girls the news that Liz would stand down for them at the wedding.

'Liz!' Keith burst out at once. 'You haven't given yourself time to think about this,' he said, the words coming out in a rush. 'You're being too hasty. Don't you realise I'm offering to share my life with you in Canada?'

'But I don't want to go to Canada!'

It was the umpteenth time she had told him, but he just wouldn't listen.

'You'd love it,' he continued, unconcerned, as if he hadn't heard. 'The houses are wooden, with big rooms. There's plenty of open space, and Lake Huron is like the sea. It's huge! The land we've got's just the place for a boat-building and repair yard.'

Liz took a deep breath and counted to ten. She was getting nowhere with him. He just couldn't understand why she wasn't eagerly agreeing with his plans.

'It all sounds very attractive, Keith, but I . . . ' But just then she was interrupted as the McDonalds' door opened and the two younger girls and their mother appeared, looking delighted. Esther was behind them.

'Oh, Liz, you're there! Thanks, lass,' Olive said. 'It's made me right happy that Sylvia's sisters will be her bridesmaids tomorrow.'

Olive sniffed, wiping moisture from her eye, and she was about to make a tearful announcement when Fiona McDonald laughed and grasped Keith's arm.

'We're not bothered about the sisterly

bit. We've got our eye on the best man!'
she giggled as Lindsey grasped his other
arm and cajoled him into joining in a
gay little dance with them.

The interruption was a relief to Liz,
although she wondered why Keith was
never so light-hearted with her.

'Well, now,' Esther broke in, 'despite
the wedding, there's still work to go to
on Saturday morning, so I think you
girls should be thinking about getting
your beauty sleep.'

As they crossed to their flat, Esther
and Liz heard the sound of the twins'
footsteps echoing up the stairs and then
they were bombarding Keith with
questions about his trip.

Liz quickly took the opportunity to
escape from Keith and went indoors
with her mother.

Once inside, she made for the big
room, and her bed — sanctuary.

She was standing holding her forehead when her mother quietly came in
after her.

'Mum, I keep telling him I don't

want to go to Canada, but he just won't listen. He keeps going on about the fortune that's just waiting to be made with their shipbuilding skills — and my expertise in pricing and sending out tenders.'

'And you're not tempted at all?' Esther asked quietly.

'No!' Liz shook her head. 'Definitely not! Do you know, he never even actually proposed marriage first? He just coolly informed me that I'm to take over the office side of this business that he and his father and uncle are setting up in Canada!'

Liz sighed again and went across the room to the large wardrobe to draw out her outfit for the wedding.

Wistfully she held it in front of her and Esther looked consideringly at the calf-length dress, fashionably flared at the hem, which Liz had copied from a model she'd seen in a shop window in Sauchiehall Street.

'You know,' her mother said, 'with my little hat and your smart court shoes and one or two other ideas I have, we should be able to make your brides-maid's dress into a nice guest's outfit.'

'You're a marvel, Mum.' Liz smiled for the first time in a week, delighted to have something to take her mind off Keith Watson.

★   ★   ★

Next day, as they did every Saturday morning, Liz and Will went down into the yard. She was glad of her hairdresser's appointment that after-noon as a stiff breeze off the river swirled clouds of dust around them.

'They're getting machines and tur-bines ready for despatch. We've got to keep the cash flow going,' Will explained as they made for the specialist sheds. 'That's one of the conditions my grandfather made when his bank gave us their backing,' he added.

'He's certainly helped the men in the yard to sleep easy at night,' Liz replied.

'And I believe you were involved?'

'Well, yes,' he said hesitantly. 'I grew up despising my grandfather. My father felt he treated my grandmother shamefully. But last week my grandfather told me his side of the story. She refused to marry him.'

As they walked on together Will related the sad love story. It seemed his grandmother had believed her poor background would hinder his grandfather's career. She had died a few years later, but Sir Edwin had never married and had continued to fund his son's education.

Normally Liz would have felt intrigued about this, especially as Will had never mentioned his background till now, but she was still preoccupied with Keith's persistence.

Will glanced at her as she walked, head down against the wind.

'I hear you've given up the bridesmaid's job,' he commented.

'Yes. Now that they approve of Bobby being the groom, Fiona and Lindsey wanted to be Sylvia's bridesmaids again,' she replied.

'I'm surprised you've allowed the McDonald girls to take over as bridesmaids when your Keith is best man.' Will grinned. 'Fiona's a real flirt.'

Liz shrugged. 'She's wasting her time. His mind is full of emigrating to Canada.'

'And you're not keen?' he guessed.

Liz sighed. 'No. My difficulty now is trying to make Keith understand that I don't want to go.'

They walked on, with shipyard noises filling the void.

'Does that mean you don't want to marry him?' Will ventured at length.

'He doesn't know that yet.' Liz sighed. 'But yes, it does.'

At this, Will perked up and a spring appeared in his step.

Nothing was said but Liz found his response strangely comforting.

'I'm going to the wedding, too,' he said shortly. 'And so is Andy Knox here.'

The young charge-hand came forward, smiling, and Liz smiled back warily, hoping he'd accepted now that she wasn't interested in him except as a friend.

'Mrs McDonald's fair pushing the boat out,' he said. 'She's found out Bobby's one in a million and she's giving the happy couple a real slap-up send off.'

'Bobby's the last one I'd have thought of as a third in the eternal triangle with Sylvia and her mother, but he's seen it through with some determination and has gone up in everyone's estimation,' Will commented to Andy.

Liz was mildly intrigued watching Will and Andy chatting amicably. It was strange how this week, after the difficult negotiations with the bank had saved the men's jobs, those who had previously distrusted Will now respected him for what he had achieved for the yard.

Will chuckled, pointing to the towering hulk of the Two-seven-two as some of the men unrolled a large white sheet over the side of the unfinished ship, with FOR SALE painted in big black letters. Then smaller sheets appeared with CREDIT TERMS, BARGAIN PRICES and TIME TO PAY on them.

Laughter bubbled up inside Liz and she leaned helplessly against Will, tears of mirth streaming down her face.

'Oh, my goodness!' she said as she eventually got her hilarity under control. 'That sounded almost like an attack of hysteria! But it was as good as a tonic.'

'Yes,' Will agreed. 'It's probably put your problems into perspective, too.'

As they picked their way back through groups of workmen laughing up at the home-made signs, Liz was silent, trying to analyse her feelings. She'd felt so safe and secure for those short moments as Will had supported her.

★ ★ ★

The wedding day dawned bright and clear and remained that way as everyone in the close busied themselves getting ready for the occasion.

The Miss Fosters and Miss Agatha, all in their wedding finery, had come up for Esther's approval of their outfits, and now they were looking on admiringly as Liz made the final adjustments to her outfit in front of the mirror.

'By, lass, you look a treat,' the older women chorused, then they all made their way downstairs before the bride and her uncle came out.

A taxi was waiting at the entrance to the close, ready to take them to the little red sandstone church in Scotstoun.

Liz was glad no-one had mentioned Keith, for he'd made no attempt to see her today.

Her hurt and confusion increased when she felt a pang at the sight of him, standing tall and handsome at Bobby's side during the service. It was painful to give up her dreams — even now when she knew that was all they had been. Nothing but fantasies!

The reception was held in the tea-room of the local bakery, which was famed for its steak pies.

Just as Liz took her place, a waitress passed her a note.

'It's from your intended,' she whispered.

With a sinking heart Liz read the brief message:

'I'll mention our forthcoming nuptials in my speech.
'Keith.'

Liz looked over to him, but he was busy with his best man's duties — engrossed in conversation with Fiona and Lindsey, the bridesmaids.

The wavering moment she'd had earlier in church turned to fury. She took a pencil from her handbag, and scribbled a few sentences on the note for the waitress to take back.

She watched his face while he read it,

saw the frostiness replace the smiles.

As her eyes bored straight through him, he glared back, then looked away. It was only then Liz noticed that Will Robertson had been closely watching their exchange . . .

Liz hardly tasted the meal, while the laughing and joking all around were merely a background noise.

Her whole body tensed when Keith rose to make his best man's speech, which was mercifully brief — and made no mention of her.

The minute the meal was finished, he was by her side, his handsome face perplexed.

'Liz! What's happened to you? Everyone expects us to get engaged.'

'I don't see why they should!' she said coolly. 'We never went out together until the week before you left, and you've only been back a week. Even your affectionate letters were written by someone else!'

'Well . . . but everyone expected we'd become a pair,' he persisted.

'Before you came home, I dreamed that, too — until I learned that you wasted a full twenty-four hours before contacting me!' She looked at him steadily.

'But my father thought we should tell Mr Wingrave about calling the baby after him ... since he's got no-one coming after him to bear his name,' Keith stammered.

'The fact that you went there first shows where I stand in your priorities. I can't be the person you truly want to marry!' Liz said evenly.

Keith looked away in sudden embarrassment, and that response made Liz certain that her suspicions were well founded.

'You've met someone else, haven't you, Keith?' she asked quietly.

When his colour rose higher she knew she'd hit the bull's-eye.

'Not really,' he mumbled. 'I only met her for a few days at my uncle's place but — '

Liz recalled Eleanor Martin's prophetic remarks on how going away from this close-knit shipbuilding community would open up new opportunities to him and change him, and she somehow gained the confidence to sound cool and businesslike. She knew, too, that this was her opportunity to cut her ties with him once and for all.

'Face it, Keith. You'd feel cheated if you went back to Canada married to me and found yourself still attracted to this other girl. Anyway,' she went on, 'if you're starting out on a new venture, you'd best be single.'

'Liz, I . . . ' he started weakly, but she calmly interrupted.

'You know what I'm saying makes sense, Keith. Let's shake hands and go on as we've always been — good friends.'

She extended her hand and he stared at it, confused for a moment, before he finally shook it.

'If that's how you want it,' he murmured.

She wanted to retort that in his heart he wanted it, too, but she simply nodded.

'That's what I want,' she echoed.

As her words sank in, he frowned and looked troubled, and kept hold of her hand.

'Liz — you've not thought this through. Let's leave it for now till you've had time to reconsider.'

She closed her eyes in disbelief but immediately felt comforted when she heard Will's steady voice beside her.

'Her answer is no, Keith!'

At Last, At Last!

By the first light of the misty October morning, Esther watched from the oriel window in the big room as Robbie reached the foot of Yarrowholm Street. He turned as usual to salute her with a raised finger to the peak of his cap.

It was his first day back after his accident, and she was grateful for his recovery.

She turned at the sound of Liz pulling back the red plush curtains in front of the set-in bed by the door before she started to make it.

'Eleanor and June's dresses for the wedding look lovely,' Esther commented. The two velvet dresses in different shades of autumn gold were hanging outside the wardrobe. 'You've worked so hard on them this last couple of week since Sylvia's wedding.'

Esther frowned a little as she watched her daughter. She felt guilty. Liz never

298

complained, yet years of handing over her wages to help Andrew qualify as a doctor had deprived her of pleasures that other young women of her age took for granted.

Esther ached for her to enjoy the kind of happiness she and Robbie had always shared.

'The last fitting was supposed to be tonight, but now June's uncle has turned up, I'm not sure,' Liz said.

'Ay,' Esther said. 'Apparently he's pleased his sister's marrying into the Burnham family. He didn't have much to do with them before.'

Before she could say more, she was interrupted by the doorbell.

'I'll go,' Liz murmured. 'It's probably Keith come to say cheerio!'

As she'd predicted it was indeed Keith waiting on the doorstep. He grinned disarmingly at her.

'I'm off to re-join my ship,' he said in an excited rush, then stopped and held up an envelope. 'And — ' he paused ' — you were right. This letter's from

Jacqueline to say she's back home in Montreal. She's waiting for me.'

'Oh, Keith, I'm really delighted for you!' Liz said sincerely.

Esther remained quiet in the bedroom, unashamedly eavesdropping, and she was delighted when she heard Keith's parting words.

'And I hope you and Will Robertson end up together. He cares for you, you know — like I do for Jacqueline. And you and I . . . we'll remain the friends we always were.'

He gave her a quick peck on the cheek and was gone.

Once Keith's footsteps were out of earshot, Liz quietly closed the door.

Esther joined her and was about to give vent to her feelings about Keith, and ask about Will, but she caught sight of the new serenity on Liz's face.

* * *

That morning Liz had a new spring in her step when she reached the office and Mr Nigel smiled as she came through the swing doors humming to herself.

'Eleanor says you've made her wedding dress by copying the new designs from Paris,' he said.

Liz still wasn't used to this more mellow Mr Nigel — even using a first name in the office!

He paused, before continuing, 'June and your brother, Andrew, seem to have become very friendly . . .'

When Liz nodded, he went on, 'Would you say an engagement and marriage are on the cards?'

Then he added quickly when he saw the alarm on her face, 'I only ask because she says she's going to stay on in the Yarrowholm Street flat after her mother and I are married. And — well, what I mean is, it hardly seems fitting for a young unmarried woman to be living on her own when there's a home with us.'

Just then, to Liz's relief, June and her mother came through the swing door.

June's eyes danced as she caught sight of Mr Nigel talking with Liz. She could guess what that was about!

June quizzed Liz later when they had a moment alone in the cloakroom and Liz assured her, 'He's genuinely concerned about you living alone. He — he wondered how things are between you and Andrew. If — you have any plans,' she added tactfully.

June gave a little chuckle.

'Andrew has told me that we won't be able to get married for perhaps four years or so,' she confessed. 'He's got to buy a car, then try to buy a practice. But I've told him I'll be saving, too, so maybe we can do it in less. After all, the flat would be a cheap first home.'

She gave a happy sigh and rushed on, 'Thank goodness you've made our dresses for the wedding. It's the best present Mummy and I could have had. That quality would have cost us a fortune, which we don't have — although I'll soon have a car!'

Liz turned from the mirror in surprise.

'How on earth will you get a car?'

'From dear old Uncle Sebastian! He can afford it! And now Mummy is marrying into the Burnhams, he's decided we're worth knowing again,' June said dryly. 'So when he asked what I'd like for my twenty-first birthday, I suggested a car! Just think, I'll be able to teach Andrew how to drive.

'Is Will due back soon?' she asked, changing the subject.

Liz shrugged. 'I'm not sure. The business he's doing for the yard has taken longer than expected but he might be back today. I'm going down to the yard with Bobby this morning.' She lowered her voice. 'It's such a relief that there's no resentment any more.'

'Will's gone up in everyone's estimation — managing to bring Burnham's back from the brink. It's obvious he's being groomed for a position on the board,' June continued. 'Bobby probably knows Will's job will be his soon.'

Liz remembered her mother hinting as much. It certainly seemed feasible in the light of recent developments in Burnham's.

★ ★ ★

Bobby turned up the collar of his brown overall coat as the ice-edged wind clipped his ears as he and Liz made their way down to the Loft.

'I wish I'd put my hat on!' he remarked.

Suddenly he grabbed her arm and pointed.

'Look, there's Will by the Two-seven-two with Mr Burnham and that banker they say is his grandfather. I wonder who the other two men are?'

Liz looked over to where the men were standing examining the towering structure of the ship's hull above them. Then she realised Will was talking to the two strangers in another language.

Bobby gave an amazed whistle.

'I didn't know Will could speak French!'

'Neither did I,' Liz replied in some amazement.

'And did you know he has an MA degree and another degree in engineering?' Bobby smiled, pleased to be the holder of such information.

Liz could only shake her head.

She stared over at Will, gesturing and explaining the different parts of the hull. It seemed Bobby was talking about a stranger, not the Will she knew, forever running his hands through his tousled, wavy hair and constantly teasing her.

Bobby laughed as he went on, 'And to think some of us thought he wasn't up to being chief cost clerk because he hadn't served his apprenticeship here! Weren't we the dopes? He's got a soft spot for you, you know,' he remarked as they walked back from the Loft.

Liz smiled politely, weary of such remarks.

When they got back to the office, Will was studying some drawings but as he glanced up and smiled quietly to her she suddenly felt almost shy of him. It was their first meeting since the night of Sylvia and Bobby's wedding, when he had confronted Keith.

★ ★ ★

Will came up behind her as she cleared her desk before lunch.

'We've got a buyer for the Two-seven-two,' he told her. 'I've been helping negotiate the sale.'

'Oh, that's wonderful!' she exclaimed.

He smiled. 'I'm pretty pleased about it myself! And there are to be some changes in the office. But let's discuss them over lunch. I spoke to your father earlier and told him you won't be home.'

'Well, if you put it like that, how can I refuse?' she said, secretly pleased that he was seeking her company.

When they left the office, her young brother Harry was standing by Will's Riley sports car, brandishing his reporter's pad.

'Will!' he called. 'There's a rumour that a ship's been sold. Is it true?'

'How on earth did you hear so quickly?' Will asked. 'The deal was only completed an hour ago.'

He opened the passenger door for Liz and waited while she got in, then he turned back to Harry.

'It's true,' he said. 'The Two-seven-two is to be completed for a new owner in Portugal. The bank gave us invaluable help in finding the contact. There will be changes, including promotions — and these will be finalised shortly.'

'And I've heard you two are about to partake of luncheon,' Harry went on, his eyes dancing with mischief. 'Would you care to expand further on the reasons, Mr Robertson?' He pointed his pad to the office windows above from where a row of white faces was watching them. 'After all, half of Burnham's drawing office are putting their own interpretation on your move-ments,' he added.

'Harry, this is business!' Liz said heatedly.

★ ★ ★

Will drove to a small hotel in Great Western Road, where they were shown to a corner table in the dining-room.

Over lunch he described the last two weeks working with his grandfather.

'There was no stopping the old boy once he got engrossed in the project,' Will enthused. 'It makes me ashamed at how he was blamed for all our troubles during my childhood. My father never said a good word about him. Of course, he was a sick man.'

Liz listened entranced as he described his childhood, being taken round Europe by his artist parents, always subsidised by his grandfather's allowance — as he'd just discovered.

Gradually Liz pieced together the story of his eighteen-year-old art student mother and his father at nineteen, eloping and cutting ties with their families.

'The more I'm with my grandfather the more I see how my father misunderstood him. My grandfather looked on my grandmother as his wife — they'd plighted their troth in the old Scots way, holding a Bible between them over the running water of a burn. My grandmother was connected to Highland tinkers, you see.'

'It's from the old handfasting custom,' Liz confirmed.

Will nodded. 'Those vows bound them, and my grandmother refused to get a written certificate. Apparently she couldn't read or write and thought it would make him a laughing stock. My grandfather has remained a one-woman man all his life.'

'When did you discover your Cunningham grandparents' existence?'

'My mother went home to them to die,' he explained. 'They never remonstrated with her, although I can understand their shock and disappointment when their only child ran off with a man who was poor in health, untrained to make a living, and illegitimate. It was a terrible stigma in those days.'

Liz could sympathise with old Mrs Cunningham, the lonely years she'd endured, while her wayward daughter lived like a gipsy, cutting her off from the love of her only grandchild.

'That's why I've always envied you having such sensible parents and close family around you,' Will said quietly.

'You'll find Costing very dull after all these high-powered shenanigans.' Liz laughed.

'Actually,' he relied slowly, 'I may be leaving Burnham's . . .'

'Why?' Liz felt as though the bottom had fallen out of her world. 'Have you had another job offer?'

'No. Burnham's have offered me promotion, but it depends on how you feel about whether I stay — or leave.'

Liz looked baffled. 'What do you mean?'

'Well, everybody except you realises

that I want the place in your affections that Keith had before he came home.'

Liz felt herself stiffen. What was he saying? She was never sure when he was teasing.

'I've been offered the position of General Manager here, but I don't want to make any decisions until I'm sure of your feelings for me.' He paused and went on awkwardly, 'I'm sorry, Liz, I'm not putting this very well . . . but I spoke to your father this morning, and he gave me permission to ask you.'

He stirred his coffee, avoiding her eyes now, and Liz felt her heart do a huge somersault.

'For over two years,' he began again, 'ever since I started with Burnham's, I've become more and more . . . ' He stopped, and bit his lip. Then he looked at her appealingly. 'I love you, Liz. Will you marry me? There — I've said it all.'

'I — I never realised . . . I don't know what to say . . . ' Liz whispered.

'How about yes?' He put his hand over hers. 'I've got to know if you could learn to love me, as I love you. But don't answer right now. Take your time to think about it.'

Liz was in a daze as they left the hotel dining-room. She knew Will's proposal was serious. He loved her. They drove back to the office in silence.

Will parked the car near the entrance and turned to look intently at her.

'Well? Do you have an answer for me, Liz?'

As he looked into her eyes, the barriers she'd built round her heart finally crumbled. She knew she wanted to spend the rest of her life with him. Wherever he wanted to go, she would be by his side.

'Yes, I'll marry you!' she told him, and saw the joy light up his face.

'Fantastic!' he shouted, and enveloped her in his arms, his lips seeking hers.

'We must make it official. I'll let your father know right away,' he said.

Liz gulped, astonished at how quickly her life had changed. She sat, still in a daze, as Will clambered out of the car.

'This meeting will last for most of the afternoon. But don't go home. Wait for me!' he ordered, his voice full of laughter and happiness. 'We'll go and look at rings on the way home.' Then he took to his heels.

Liz got out of the car in a sort of trance and walked slowly up the stairs into the office, her mind reeling.

As applause greeted her from the assembled female staff including Fiona and Lindsey, she stared uncomprehendingly at them.

'Will told us your good news on his way through to the meeting,' Eleanor Martin told her, enveloping her in a warm hug. 'It's just wonderful.'

★　★　★

It was past stopping-time when Will's meeting finished, and Liz was thankful to sit in the empty office, gathering her thoughts.

She was composed when Mr Nigel

came out and invited her to join Will in the meeting and receive the Board's good wishes on their engagement.

A little over an hour later they were in Yarrowholm Street, Liz with a sparkling three-diamond ring on the third finger of her left hand.

The whole family was waiting, the table laid for a party. All the neighbours, except Eddie Watson, were waiting for them, too.

'Mum, how on earth did you manage all this?' Liz gasped.

Her mother laughed. 'I had some willing helpers. The two Miss Fosters — and Olive McDonald and Sylvia — even Miss Agatha!'

Her father dispensed whisky to the men, and glasses of sherry to the ladies, then raised his glass in a toast.

'We wish Will and Liz God's blessing, a long life, and much happiness together — just like her mother and I have enjoyed for nigh on twenty-seven years!'

Will stood beside Liz, his arm

possessively about her shoulders.

'This is the best engagement party I've ever had,' he quipped with a twinkle in his eye. 'And the only one!' he whispered in her ear. 'I'm like my grandfather! A one-woman man!'

Liz smiled up at him, her heart bursting with happiness.

THE END

VISIONS OF THE HEART

Christine Briscomb

When property developer Connor Grant contracted Natalie Jensen to landscape the grounds of his large country house near Ashley in South Australia, she was ecstatic. But then she discovered he was acquiring — and ripping apart — great swathes of the town. Her own mother's house and the hall where the drama group met were two of his targets. Natalie was desperate to stop Connor's plans — but she also had to fight the powerful attraction flowing between them.

THE PERFECT GENTLEMAN

Liz Pedersen

When Laura agrees to help Anthony Christopher to deceive his family she has no idea how far the web of intrigue will extend, or how it will alter her life. His family is as unpleasant as he promised, but Laura drives away from his funeral thinking she has escaped their malicious clutches. However, this is not so. James Christopher is determined to discover what was behind his cousin's precipitate marriage. He despises Laura and hates the fact that he is attracted to her.

YESTERDAY'S LOVE

Stella Ross

Jessica's return from Africa to claim her inheritance of 'Simon's Cottage', and take up medicine in her home town, is the signal for her past to catch up with her. She had thought the short affair she'd had with her cousin Kirk twelve years ago a long-forgotten incident. But Kirk's unexpected return to England, on a last-hope mission to save his dying son, sparks off nostalgia. It leads Jessica to rethink her life and where it is leading.

ZABILLET OF THE SNOW

Catherine Darby

For Zabillet, a young peasant girl growing up in the tiny French village of Fromage in the mid-fourteenth century, a respectable marriage is the height of her parents' ambitions for her. But life is changing. Zabillet's love for a handsome shepherd is tested when she is invited to join the La Neige household, where her mistress, Lady Petronella, has plans for her grandson, Benet. And over all broods the horror of the Great Death that claims all whom it touches.

PERILOUS JOURNEY

Caroline Joyce

After the execution of Charles I, Louisa's Royalist father considers it too dangerous for her to stay in England and arranges for her to go to the Isle of Man with Armand de la Tremouille, the nephew of the island's Royalist Governor. Their ship is boarded by Parliamentarians who plan to sail for Ireland, but a storm causes them to be shipwrecked on the Calf of Man. Magnus Stapleton, the Parliamentarian chief, becomes infatuated with Louisa, but she has fallen in love with Armand.

THE GYPSY'S RETURN

Sara Judge

After the death of her cruel father, Amy Keene's stepbrother and stepsister treated her just as badly. Amy had two friends, old Dr. Hilland and the washerwoman, Rosalind, with her fatherless child Becky. When Rosalind falls ill, Amy is entrusted with a letter to be given to Becky on her marriage. When the letter's contents are discovered, it causes Amy both mental and physical suffering and sets the seal of fate upon Rosalind's gypsy friend, Elias Jones.